IMPACT

HALEY JENNER

Edited by
ELLIE MCLOVE

Warning: This book contains topics that may upset or offend readers, especially those who have previously experienced sexual violence.

COPYRIGHT

DEDICATION

to the warriors; the ones who have had their choice to say no
stolen from them

ACKNOWLEDGMENTS

Acknowledgments, oh, how we've missed you. These few pages in our books are some of, if not *the*, most important words in each and every one of our novels. Why? Because it's here, in this collection of words - that will likely never be enough - we get to thank each and every person that has once again helped us see our dream come to life with the publication of another story.

Zoe and Tripp's story burst into our minds one night and from that moment, no other story could gain traction. It was them and only them. They wanted their love story to grace the pages of a book and who are we to deny their wish?

To our families, thank you for enduring through our incessant need to hide away and write. Our love for you knows no bounds. Your support through this journey we're taking inspires us to keep going. Thank you for loving us as hard as you do and supporting us in the same way.

As always, Ellie McLove... we could not do this without you. Thank you seems such a mediocre word considering the extent of how much our gratefulness extends to you and your presence in our life. Your support is unwavering, like the love we have for you. Thank you for polishing our words, for the love you pour into designing our covers, for continuing on this HJ journey no matter how painful we are at times. We look forward to a time when we can sit and enjoy a meal at the Waterloo (yes, H will likely order the pork tacos, *again*) and talk shit about who could outrun a coyote and who would push who in front of who to save themselves. (Even if we are trapped next to a screaming toddler on a fourteen-hour flight.)

Michelle Clay and Annette Brignac, you've both been an absolute GODSEND with this release. Life definitely got in the way for us this year, but your input into the HJ world made everything SO much easier. THANK YOU. Words don't seem enough, but we adore you both and our gratitude knows no bounds. We look forward to the day we can squeeze you both. (Also, Michelle how did this *not* happen at BBTB.) Margaritas on us.

Serena. Babe. Words can't express the excitement we felt when you messaged us to ask for an early copy of IMPACT. Truth be told, we were worried about this book (read H was worried about this book) – it's so very different to what we normally delve deep into when writing, and we weren't one hundred percent sure how it would be received. You alleviated that. Completely. Living through you as you read this story was a moment we'll cherish forever. Giddy smiles and high fives were in full flight that day. Love you. We promise to throw anal in the next book *just* for you.

To our review team. How many times can we say 'WE LOVE YOU' until you know it's forever and unyielding? We're grateful to each and every one of you and we mean that from the very bottom of our black little hearts. Thank you for taking this journey with us.

To every blogger that has taken a chance on a HJ novel. We couldn't do this without you. Thank you for every share, every comment, every like. We *see* you. We *appreciate* you. You rock. Thank you for sparking a light of excitement over the books you read through this community. Much love to each and every one of you.

Authors. Man, this community continues to blow our minds. The support that is unwavering among indie authors makes it something really special to be a part of. You're all amazing. Your words. Your dedication. Your love. You inspire us every day.

Group Therapy. We don't even have words to express the love we have for you babes. Lord. We could go on forever. We've said it before, we'll continue to say it. Our reader group is our *most* favorite place. You bring smiles to our faces, you make us laugh. Your love warms our hearts. Thank you for being the *most* supportive collective of people we've ever known. Authoring can be a lonely ride (even with two of us), but you make our worlds feel full. We love you.

Last, but most important, our readers. You are everything and we love you. It blows our mind each and every time you pick up one of our books, more when you love it. Like, is this really the life we're living? People not only reading our words but *digging* them. Thank you, thank you, thank you for giving life to our dream. We're eternally grateful.

I know we said grateful through that section no less than one million times, but go with it, yeah? That's how we feel. Every day.

We hope you enjoy Tripp and Zoe's story. It's an important one. We'd also love you times a million if you could leave a review. We love hearing your thoughts.

Much love, as always, H and J xx

IMPACT PLAYLIST

Bad Reputation, Shawn Mendes
Dark Times, The Weekend, Ed Sheeran
Lie To Me, 5 Seconds of Summer
Lips On You, Maroon 5
Remedy, Adele
If You Ever Wanna Be In Love, James Bay
Life Support, Sam Smith
Broken, Jess Glynne
Broken, Isak Danielson
Bad At Love, Halsey
Overcome, Live
Everybody Hurts, R.E.M.
Take Me Home, Jess Glynne
Praying, Kesha
Skyscraper, Demi Lovato
I'll Stand By You, Pretenders
Love Me Anyway, Pink (feat. Chris Stapleton)

IMPACT Playlist

ONE

Defeat. Surrender.

Varying ends of a depressing spectrum. *Polar* opposites. One signifying greater power. Strength. *Winning.* The other its counterpart. *Resignation.* A white flag waving so loudly it's a perfect symbol of your own submission.

Memories tend to be cataloged by reminders, the familiarity your senses recognize pulling past experiences back into the forefront of your mind. Voluntary or not, it doesn't matter. A smell, a taste, the feeling of touch, something you can see. They're appreciations your mind collects over time, building your life experience. Be it positive or negative.

I'd imagine most people would smell the cedar wood here in this room. The potent odor that tickles your nostrils, lingering with importance and command. For me, the smell is repugnant. *Suffocating.* One that will haunt me for the remainder of my days. So thick with my *own* defeat, with failure, I can't even manage to pull a full breath.

My ears feel hollow. Comparable to the feeling of being submerged in water, voices above nothing but a dull echo.

The scrape of a chair, the clearing of a throat... all too far away, yet closer than I'd care for them to be.

Inhaling heavily through my mouth, I taste the bitterness of my own remise. My hands shake, and I clench them tightly around the brittle sheets of paper clasped within my damp palms.

Smoothing the crinkled lines against the podium, I blink forcibly in an attempt to focus on the scratch of blue pen marked messily along the lines.

My heart is screaming at me to stop. To walk away. Leave the chips to fall where they may. *I'm not strong enough* my heart insists. Not to continue along this path. *We just want to sleep* it says. Crawl into the warmth of my bed and *never* leave. We'll be safe there.

Safe.

But I've yet to hand over the final sliver of strength left in my mind. I'm clinging to that like a lifeline, it's letting me breathe, if just for now. I don't doubt that after today I would've used that up too. My mind henceforth as empty as my body, as my heart currently feels.

"Eight months ago." My words feel like stripped metal on my vocal cords. Jagged and useless. I clear my throat, refusing to look anywhere but at the words before me. "I had my whole life ahead of me. I was young. I was happy," I continue. "Eight months ago, my body was *mine*. My *mind* was *mine*." My voice shakes right before it cracks and I pause, clenching my teeth against the tremor in my jaw. I bite my lip, silencing the indelicate sob fighting to escape. Hints of it succeed, choking out in a stuttered breath.

"Moments of that night are faded, hazy in parts. But there are fragments, flashes, minutes that are so very clear. They're my own living nightmare, and no matter how hard I try... I can't escape."

I glance up then, seeking refuge from the judge. A middle-aged white man with hair the color of snow. My lawyer assured me his allotment to my case was a good thing. His history, his *long* history, shows a clear bias toward women's rights.

The weathered lines of his face give nothing away. Only watching on impassively as I speak, but I take solace in the kindness in his eyes, encouraging me forward.

"You took liberty on my body that wasn't yours to take, but what I think you failed to realize, or possibly you didn't care," I shrug to myself, my shoulders remaining bunched near my neck in defense. "Is that in that decision, you stole the liberty of my mind. *Your* actions, *your* decision... it now controls my life."

I pause, needing a second to gather my composure. Inhaling deeply, I roll my shoulders, releasing them from the bind of my neck.

"My life is now an ode to what you stole. First, it was my body, my right to say no. Then you murdered my dignity. I realized that more as I lay on a hospital bed, my legs open as doctors poked and prodded my already violated body."

Images of that moment choose to flood my mind, and I choke on my breath. Bile rushes up my throat, but I swallow the acidity and the burn of the memories back down.

"You stripped away my feeling of safety. I panic in crowds, but I'm *petrified* to be alone. Which means I no longer know where I fit in this world.

"I have a scar on my inner thigh. One you gave me. A bite mark so brutal it remains imprinted in my skin like a tattoo.

It's the only reminder I'm shockingly thankful for because it led to your arrest. It's ugly and it will likely stay that way forever. Which is fitting because it's now how I feel as a person. Ugly. Scarred. Damaged."

I can feel his eyes burning a hole in the side of my face. The liquid stare that wakes me every night; screaming, sweating, and confident I'm ready to die.

"I Googled how long it takes skin to regenerate. The internet says twenty-seven days. It doesn't seem like much, but for me, it felt like an eternity before the skin that you had touched would be gone from my body. What I didn't know was that your touch had burnt itself into my soul. So even if I could shed my skin in the way I hoped, it wouldn't have made a difference."

I listen as the court stenographer records my statement, word for word. The soft *tap tap* of fingers bracketing my words.

"I see you in every man I come across. The mailman. The police officer who took my statement. The elderly man who walks his dog every morning and every afternoon by my house. They're all you. I fear you. I fear them. I feel unsafe. I don't leave my house. Not unless I'm forced to. My life has changed irrevocably from the moment you made the choice to enter my body without consent. I live my life alone and imagine I always will. Interaction with others is now too difficult. Can they see it? My shame. Do they know how disgusting I am? How *dirty?*"

A tear falls from my lashes and I wipe at it quickly, annoyed that he'll see me cry again.

"Eight months ago I had my whole life ahead of me." I force myself to look at him. The blink of time that our eyes connect enough to open the floodgates as my tears begin a continuous journey down my face. "Now I've pushed away every friend I've ever had. I quit my job. I ended a relationship that up until you, made me feel like the most special person in the world. Now I feel like a nobody. I have no direction because I'm lost and no matter which direction I turn, it's *you* that I come up against."

He stares at me blankly, the picture of perfection in his chair.

"Eight months ago I was young. I was happy. Now, most days I feel ready to die. My self-worth is so low I consider that the world would likely be a better place without me. Happiness is a memory I can no longer recall. I can't remember feeling anything but the emptiness I'm now consumed by. You stole my life, Miller Jacobs. You stole my life when you violated my body. You'll leave prison one day and live your life. There will be roadblocks for you, I'm sure, but I'll live in the prison of my mind for eternity. I curse you for that, for making me both the victim and the sentenced."

Folding my paper, I hold it in my shaking hands. Looking away from my rapist, I focus back on the judge. Knowing that I just handed over the final thread of strength I had been clinging to. I was right. From the very tips of my toes to the hairs on my head, I feel devoid, empty. Zoe Lincoln no longer exists. Not in this world. She gave the last piece of her soul in a show of strength, but it took everything from her in the process.

TWO

four years later

"MARCO." I speak loud enough to be heard over the consistent chatter of the coffee shop. Sliding an Americano over to the guy that steps up, avoiding eye contact and moving my hand away quick enough that our skin won't accidentally touch. He thanks me, but I ignore him, turning back to the screen.

This is how I spend the remainder of my shift. How I spend *every* shift. Avoiding actual human interaction where possible. People with an insight into my history may think I'm scared, uncomfortable, frightened of others. I *somewhat* disagree. My hesitancy stems from the infuriating characteristic of human nature that requires people to *know* you. People are fundamentally intrusive. I don't like that. My past is my business. If I choose to share any part of myself, it's on my terms. *Not* by any possibility on theirs. Not anymore.

Folding my apron neatly into a square, I slide it into my

bag, thankful that my torturous five-hour shift is now complete.

"Taylor."

That's me. Taylor. More, it's who I identify as now. Taylor Smith. Non-existent, up until four years ago anyway.

I glance up from my bag, looking to Mya expectantly.

"Right. You don't really talk." Her eyes widen sarcastically, but she smiles, all the same, sighing. "You should come out with me and my friends sometime. You seem a little, I don't know, closed off. You need to loosen up."

She doesn't fold her apron. She balls it up, wrapping the tie strings around the ball before shoving it in her bag. It irritates me. More than it should. Granted, I know that she's taking it home to wash it, but still. It just demonstrates how she'd live her life. Chaotic, rushed. There'd be no order, no structure.

"We're heading to Keybar tonight. On Thirteenth," she clarifies unnecessarily.

"Appreciate the offer, Mya, but clubs aren't really my thing."

"*No,*" she feigns shock, a genuine smile touching her lips.

I return the gesture.

"Come. It'll be fun. It's not really a *club*. Totally lowkey."

My head begins shaking before she's finished her sentence.

"*Please,*" she begs, and I have to give it to her, she's persistent. I have no clue why. We're not friends. We don't chat. In fact, I'm quite positive this interaction right now is the most words we've ever exchanged. "I've got this friend, he'd be *so* into you."

"Not interested," I shut her down abruptly causing her eyebrows to draw together.

"No need to be rude. I was just saying he's a nice guy—"

"And I told you I'm not interested," I cut her off impolitely.

She mutters under her breath, retrieving her bag.

"Look, Mya," I start, waiting for her to look at me. "I'm sorry. I just... I'm not interested in meeting anyone."

She watches me for a beat, sympathy cloaking her eyes like curtains, sliding all the way across to shroud them in pity. "Bad breakup?"

I want to laugh. If only. "Yeah," I lie. "Something like that."

"I get it." She waves me off. "Maybe another time."

She turns and walks away before I can reject her again and I exhale heavily, following her exit from the storeroom.

"It's not the *worst* idea, Zoe."

I stare at Hannah through the screen of my Mac, shock forcing my eyebrows to my hairline.

There's a smudge on my screen, blurring the line of her eye and I lean forward to rub it away.

"Not the club," she clarifies, playing with the pen in her

hand. "Don't get me started on the number of triggers that would cause. Baby steps. I just mean *getting out.*"

I shift on my couch, pulling my legs under my butt. "I get out." The defensive tone isn't lost to my ears.

Hannah smiles. "Zoe, working three days a week in a coffee shop to pretend you're engaging in human interaction is *not* getting out. How many customers did you actually converse with today?"

I look away, patting Potter's fur, making him purr.

"My point exactly. The job was a great idea, Zoe," she reassures. "It got you comfortable catching public transportation, being around crowds. The next step is to interact. Converse with other people."

I nod. "There *is* a book club advertised through the book store I visit... they meet once a month on a Saturday morning."

"I think it's a great idea," she encourages. "That's your homework for the next month. Actually committing to attend *and* following through."

"Okay," I agree easily.

"Okay?"

I bite back my laughter. "I said okay."

The clock on my mantel ticks by in a solid and consistent beat, counting the seconds of silence that hangs between us.

"How are the nightmares?"

I cross my arms over my chest in defense. A tick that seems to have become a habit every time she brings up my broken sleep.

"Infrequent," I confess. "Depends on the day."

Hannah contemplates me for a moment, placing her pen neatly on her desk to lean closer. "The thing with PTSD is that there's always going to be triggers. The cognitive processing therapy we worked on when you were still living here was incredibly successful in moving you past your stuck points. The self-blame. We've combated and overcome your thought process that *you* could've done something differently."

The months following the incident, I was consumed with self-loathing. I wholeheartedly blamed myself. I would spend days on end *obsessing* over everything I could have done differently. How easy it would've been for me to avoid what happened to me. It was the hardest thing I've ever had to come to terms with, but with Hannah's guidance, I got to a point where I understood that I had no blame in Miller's actions. They were his and his alone.

That acceptance aside, I've still yet to move past the trauma associated with the attack. The moments that come so out of the blue, I feel like I'm thrown back to that night, useless to fight off the fear of my own memories.

"What you're now ready to overcome are the intrusive thoughts that convince you it's going to happen again, that every man you come in contact with is capable of what Miller was. You're ready to live again, and that's a big step."

"Feels impossible." My confession feels choked out of my closing throat.

"So did coming to terms with the fact that your attack wasn't your fault. You made such great progress in the years following his arrest, the relapse in your fear is perfectly under-standable. It's normal, Zoe. Your attacker was released back into society. His threat, in your mind, was reignited. Your peace will come, it all just takes time. You're still continuing with your mindfulness, your meditation?"

"Yeah," I confirm. "Every night. Every morning."

"Good," she praises, pleased by my commitment.

I like Hannah Blackhaus. She was the first therapist I met following the incident. We connected. Well enough that when I left Charlottesville behind, I reached out after I started having panic attacks after Miller's release.

Three years. That's all he served. Good behavior or something ridiculous like that. If I wasn't so broken by his actions, it'd be comical. A man took liberty on my body, he forced himself inside of me, and three years of *good* behavior in an environment he had no choice but to adhere to the rules, and he's rewarded with his freedom. It doesn't matter that I'm still stuck in the prison of my mind, a sentence handed down by him.

Hannah would be a little over forty I'd guess. Blonde hair bobbed around the cool tone of her skin. Non-descript in appearance, purposefully I assume. Everything from her voice, to her appearance, to her demeanor is subtle. Subdued almost. She speaks in a quiet, almost monotone way, the sound soft and calming like the ocean. Her hair is always the same, her face free of makeup, clothes only ever natural hues of grey, beige, and white. Even her gestures aren't overtly showy, her hands and face always moving in a measured way.

Hannah Blackhaus has built herself into someone you feel comfortable in trusting. She's not threatening in *any* way. She's a balm. A person, without conscious effort, you open yourself up to. Comfortable to share the darkest parts of your soul and even her streamlined self doesn't balk at you. She accepts, targets those twisted knots of who you are and makes it her mission to unfurl those parts closing you off.

"I started running," I offer. "Just at the gym. I can't bring myself to run through Central Park. But I run now, a few times a week. It seems to regulate my stress levels."

A look of pride touches Hannah's smile and my shoulders lift, a confidence I haven't felt in over four years filling my chest.

"Zoe..." She pauses. "You've come so far. It's so nice to see."

I feel like a fraud. I want to tell her that I'm still a broken shell of who I used to be. That all these *mechanisms* I use to survive the day are stupid, menial.

I shouldn't be afraid to talk to another human for fear they might ask me a personal question.

I shouldn't stand against the corner of the door on the subway to make sure I don't feel trapped by another human, knowing escape is right at my back.

I shouldn't refuse eye contact with any man for fear they might be him.

But I do. I do it all. Suffering through each day, surviving because I can't find it in myself to give up.

"Our time is about up." She checks her watch. "Remember your deep breathing. The unfortunate thing about triggers, Zoe, is that they're always going to be here. You're taking the right steps to ensure their effect isn't as heightened as they have been in the past. But in the moments your meditation and mindfulness *don't* work, *breathe.*" She demonstrates unnecessarily, inhaling a full breath through her nostrils, her palm moving up her body as her lungs fill. She releases it heavily through her mouth, her palm pushing downward with the deflation of her lungs.

I find myself following her movements, my body relaxing with the deep and purposeful intakes of air.

"Keep your talisman with you at all times, easily accessible." She waits for me to nod.

"YOU NEED A TALISMAN."

"A talisman?" I query, pulling my coat farther around my body.

Hannah shifts on her couch. "It won't work for everyone. But it's like an amulet, a protective object."

A dark brow rises in disbelief and she laughs. "I'm not suggesting magic can work you through this, Zoe. I'm talking about an object to ground you. Something that holds significance to you. A ring, a necklace, a coin, anything *that reminds you of who you are, who you* were *before the sexual assault began defining you."*

I consider her request.

"Don't overthink it, a simple item that reminds you of everything in this life you still *have."*

"The queen is the most powerful piece on the board, Zoe," my dad explains. "Remember that. Always. She's formidable."

"I have something," I declare confidently.

"Perfect. Keep it on your person always. Hold it in your hand when you feel panicked. Breathe, remember why that piece is important to you."

"YOU'RE DOING WELL, ZOE," Hannah breaks me from my memories. "You should be proud. Your strength is fighting through. It's there, we just need to nurture it back to the surface."

"Same time next month?"

She smiles. "Remember your homework. Book club, sign up. Speak to you in a few weeks. You know I'm here if you need anything in between."

I wave, leaning forward to end the Skype call. I close my laptop, my eyes skating across the quiet room for a solid ten minutes, my mind a blank canvas. It's common for me to feel this way after my session. A mixture of numb and calm. I can't tell you if my calmness is a result of feeling numb, my emotions shut off to a point that a feeling of peace settles inside of me. Or if it's the opposite, I'm calm to a point that the hurricane of feelings have been subdued. Either way, I like it.

It's not saying there aren't sessions where Hannah pushes me to a point that I feel as raw, as bare, as vulnerable as I did that night and the eight torturous months to follow. They definitely pop up more often than I'd like, and I don't like them so much in the moment, no matter how much better I feel the days following.

My phone rings like clockwork and I roll my eyes at Potter who doesn't see because he's too consumed with licking his paw to offer me the moral support I purchased him for. Fucking cats.

"Hi, Mom," I answer the call, standing to move around the apartment.

Steps. They say you need ten thousand a day. Do you know how hard that is? It's okay when I'm working at the coffee shop, constantly on the move. But my *real* job has me sitting on my ass for hours on end.

I'm an illustrator for children's books. I sit down for *hours* sketching, shading, coloring. My hands ache, and my butt tends to numb out after an hour. When I break, I walk, round and round my apartment like a psych patient talking to walls. Which, I'm not ashamed to admit, I also do. Friends are limited, and my walls don't judge. They like me here. Hiding from the cruel world.

"Zoe, sweetie. Dad's here, too."

"Hi, Dad."

Potter sits up at my voice, watching on, unimpressed, as I pace the apartment. Offended by my constant moving, he shifts, giving me his back before settling back into sleep.

"I can't see her," Dad mumbles.

"We're not on the face call, Richard," Mom's voice barks back, and I leave them to argue it out for another minute before Dad's voice carries through the line again.

"Zoe, we can't hear you. Are you there?"

"Yeah, guys," I sigh. "I'm here."

"How are you, sweetie?"

"I'm good, Dad," I offer quietly, working to calm the restlessness in his tone.

"Are you sure? You're so far away. I worry. Manhattan is so busy..."

I've had this same conversation every week since I moved away three years ago. Now, I'm no mathematician, but I'm guessing that my dad and I have had this conversation at *least* a hundred and fifty times.

"Dad," I stop him. "I promise. I'm doing really well. In fact, even Hannah commented on how far I'm coming along in our session just now."

"She did?" Mom asks, surprised.

"Appreciate the vote of confidence, Mom."

She *hmphs*. "I didn't mean it like that. You rarely speak

about your sessions with Hannah. I'm glad you're still keeping them up."

I swallow, rolling my shoulders in discomfort. "I stopped for a while," I confess. "But I felt stuck. I wasn't moving forward. So I called her."

"You were ready," Dad praises.

"Yeah," I agree. "I guess."

"How's the coffee shop?"

Turning on my feet and moving back across the apartment, I place them on speaker, holding the phone at my side. "It's there."

"How are your friends?"

My feet stop. Immediately. As though moving would take away from the lie that I've built about my social circle.

"They're good," I fib. "In fact, I might head out with Mya from work tonight."

I can hear Mom smile four hundred miles away. "Oh, sweetie. That's great. We'd love to meet her when we visit next."

"Umm.... Yeah. We could maybe organize that," I cringe. "When are you visiting?"

"Oh, no set plans," my dad answers. "Maybe Christmas."

I breathe a sigh of relief. Not that I don't miss my parents, they're wonderful people. They're just so... overbearing. They mean well, but, even with their good intentions, they make everything worse. I'm more on edge than ever.

"What are you working on at the moment?"

I'm grateful for the change in subject, and for the next forty-five minutes, I update them on my schedule for work. Mom, bless her, pretends to be interested, but she could never get her head around the fact that I get paid to 'color in.'

We end the call on I love yous and promises to speak 'same time next week.'

Throwing my phone on the couch, I check my Fitbit, fist bumping myself for adding two and a half thousand steps to my count.

Only seven and a half thousand to go.

THREE

The book store smells like you'd imagine. Like worn pages of an aged paperback, even though the stacked shelves are filled with new editions, freshly printed copies ready for purchase. I inhale deeply like I would a library book, ingesting the magic of each and every story within these walls on a wide smile.

I'm early. My anxiety having spiked to a point that I left my house an hour before I needed to. I've spent the last two days going over every possible scenario in my head.

Arriving late, having every single person stop to stare directly at me and expect me to awkwardly introduce myself to the entire group. Sharing titbits about myself as an *icebreaker*.

Arriving on the completely wrong day and sitting there for an hour, having people stare at me awkwardly while I wait for a group that is actually meeting Sunday and *not* Saturday.

Turning up to a group of only men.

It took me twenty-four hours to come to the realization that if I walk in, early or late, and I don't feel comfortable, that

I could just... *leave.* These people don't know me. Won't know my name. Does it *really* matter if I humiliate myself?

"Looking for anything in particular?"

I turn at the soft-spoken voice. It belongs to a young woman, likely my age. Standing at least a head shorter than me, her messy blonde curls are piled up on top of her head, gifting her a few extra inches of height. She's friendly, open, an ingrained want to help written all over her face.

I force my lips to tip up, a smile stretching over my closed lips. "I'm okay. Just browsing while I kill some time."

She nods. "No worries, give me a yell if you need a hand. I'll be here for another forty-five." She checks her watch, smiling on a shrug of her shoulders before moving away.

I watch the ease in which she moves. She doesn't have to force a smile at anyone. It's automatic, genuine happiness to greet strangers. Her feet carry her around the store in a dance, swift and graceful. Tendrils of her hair fall out only to be pinned back in. Fingernails painted a soft pink, a stark and obvious difference to the chipped, and chewed line of mine.

She's a complete and miserable reminder of everything I'm not. *Alive.*

I shake off my melancholy, turning back to the rows of books, brushing my fingers along the spines in longing.

Stepping into the Starbucks, I pause at the door, my eyes tracking the room in search of anyone that screams book club. Is that a thing? I'm generalizing, I know. I'm just hoping there's a small giveaway to stop me from humiliating myself.

The blonde from Book Culture sits by herself, a group of tables haphazardly pulled together around her, her nose stuck in a book. There's a furrow to her brow, a look of concentration as she reads, the smile of her lips a complete juxtaposition.

The door touches my back, reminding me I've stopped directly in front of it, and I shift to the side, mumbling my apology to the older woman who walks past me.

"For someone who works in a book store." She approaches the blonde, voice carrying over the bustle of space. "You're the only one who *never* finishes the book before we meet. Explain that to me, would ya?"

"Hi, Vera." She rolls her eyes, closing her paperback. "For your information, I *have* read it. I was just rehashing a chapter I happened to enjoy."

I step backward, their ease of comradery as intimidating as it is enviable. Turning, I reach for the door, but Hannah's voice storms through my ears, and I pause.

Breathe.

Exhaling on a drawn-out blink, I crack my neck in an attempt to ease the discomfort of my body. If anyone notices my mini-meltdown they don't comment, hell they barely offer me a second glance and my nerves begin to dissipate.

Hand pulling back, I tuck it into my jacket, my fist clenching and unclenching to relieve the remnants of my freak out.

I force myself to take the necessary steps to reach the

table. Counting each step. It's a habit, one I can't seem to break. A compulsion to ensure I'm acutely aware of how fast I can escape should the need arise.

"Hi," I speak, sounding as hesitant and unsure as I feel.

"Hi," Vera responds.

"Random question... Are you guys a part of the book club advertised in Book Culture's window?"

"Not so random. In actuality, it's a rather appropriate question," she continues oddly. "I'm Vera. Will you be joining us?"

Glancing between their smiling faces, I swallow my apprehension. "If that's okay?"

"We'd love you to join us. Hi, I'm Quinn," the blonde stands, offering her hand. "We met in the book store."

"I remember," I reply, reluctantly taking her hand.

I choose a seat next to Quinn before Vera can offer her hand or worse, try and hug me. It would be nice if I could settle in before offending someone with my adversity to touch.

"What's your name, honey?"

I laugh uncomfortably, cursing myself for how out of practice with human interaction I am. "Oh, sorry. I'm Taylor."

"Nice to meet you. As I said, I'm Vera, the grandma of the group."

Quinn scoffs. "Don't mind her. She just turned forty and she's not coping with it. I'm gonna order my coffee before the horde arrives."

She wanders off, and Vera stands to follow her. "I'm gonna do the same. What can I get you, honey? First time. On me."

I move to argue, but she shakes her head. "Make it easier

on the awkwardness of us both. We'll keep going back and forth. Just let me buy you a coffee."

I appreciate her graceless warmth, the openness in her character. A sense of ease flows through my veins. "Iced coffee, no milk, thank you."

She doesn't reply. No *You're welcome* or smile in response to my word of thanks.

I like her. A lot, and I find myself smiling unconsciously.

By the time Quinn and Vera arrive back at the table, four more people have sat down.

One woman doesn't speak. At all. I'm not sure if it's by choice or a medical condition that stops her, but she makes her presence known, staring at me without blinking. It's disconcerting in the most horrible of ways, and if I wouldn't make a spectacle of myself, I'd likely leave. I settle for turning away from her stare instead.

A set of twins sit alongside Vera's seat, identical except for the fact that one of them has bright pink hair, three rings in her nose and a tattoo of a tiny rose under her left eye. They introduce themselves as Rose and Tamra, surprisingly, Rose *isn't* the one with the tattoo. They quickly fall into conversation amongst themselves, forgetting the rest of us and making me more acutely aware of the lady still burning holes in the side of my face.

"Sucks you can't smoke weed in here." The fourth addition sits beside me. "Hey. Don't mind Joanie, she's a little intense to begin with. You're new. She's just trying to psych you out. I'm Rae." She goes to offer her hand, watching closely to see the imperceptible widening of my eyes. Pulling it back, she leans across the table flicking Tamra's ear. "You don't like to be touched. Understood, and respected. Hey, babe." She transfers her attention to a bristling Tamra.

Sighing, she falls back into her seat. "Tamra hasn't spoken to me in a month. Not since our last meeting. She didn't appreciate my opinion on happily ever afters in romance novels."

"I'm Taylor," I introduce myself. "What was your opinion on happily ever afters?"

This conversation topic piques the rest of the table, conversation ceasing.

"I was in the minority."

"You were the *only*," Tamra bites out.

"I feel that not every romance novel needs hearts and roses at the end. I enjoy books that end where everyone is heartbroken."

I consider Rae for a beat, my gaze cataloging her appearance. She's tall and thin. A delicate shade of amber to her skin, face free of makeup, lined with a dusting of dark freckles along her cheeks. Her lips are the color of salmon; not quite pink, not quite orange, a light shade between the two. But they're big. Full, almost swollen in their puffiness. She's of Asian descent, her dark brown eyes striking on her face, similar to her lips; consequently too big for her face. But it all fits. She's exquisite. Her hair is the darkest shade of black I've ever seen, cut short, flying in every direction on top of her head.

"You get used to looking at her." A voice travels from down the table, and I startle at the sound, embarrassed at being caught.

"I'm sorry." I offer Rae a quick glance, but she shrugs. "I

look like an Asian Disney princess, with a mohawk and leather jacket, I get it."

It's only then that I realize it was Joanie who had spoken, a soft English accent dripping from her words.

"What do you think, Taylor?" she tests, oblivious to my shock at her speaking. "Happily ever afters... yay or nay?"

All sets of eyes fall on me, and I shift uncomfortably in my seat.

"Umm..." I clear my throat. "I would have to agree with Rae?" My words come out like a question. "I... life isn't always a fairy tale. It's nice when books paint that reality."

"*Yassss,*" Rae hollers, hand slamming down on the table in victory.

Sipping my iced coffee, I attempt to hide my smile.

"Interesting," Joanie quips. "I placed you as a romantic."

I bark out a laugh. "Definitely not."

"Sorry I'm late." A man in his early twenties throws his bag onto the table. "Fucking people everywhere. Remind me why I live here again?"

"More cock," Rae offers, and he clicks his fingers in her direction.

"True dat, sister."

Now the *sister* comment could be wholly and solely a term of endearment for a friend or based on the fact that they look eerily similar, he could literally mean Rae is his sister. I'm guessing the latter.

His hair is bleached to an inch of its life, combed to the side with a prominent part cut along his scalp. Like Rae, his eyes are dark, shade to be determined due to the fact that he's standing too far away for me to accurately call at this moment. They're not big like Rae's, but still striking. Skin tone the same, he shares her freckles, only his decorate the bridge of his nose. His lips are even thicker than Rae's, if that's possible. He, like her, is remarkable to look at.

"Oooooh." He looks at me, completely comfortable with my gawking. "New meat. Hi, I'm Dex."

"Taylor," I greet quietly.

"Is it rude of me to tell you that your name doesn't suit you?" He slides into a chair, readjusting the short sleeves of his hideously patterned shirt that on him somehow works.

"She does look like she'd have a *prettier* name," Joan adds without offense. "Not that Taylor *isn't* pretty, it's unisex though."

Which is why I chose it, I answer internally.

"Mm," Dex agrees, looking to Joan before looking to me once again. "I expected something more feminine. Also, you're hot AF. FYI."

"Thanks?" I drawl out uncomfortably.

"Prickly when offered a compliment. Interesting."

"Not prickly," I combat. "Just not a fan of attention. Also, do you always speak in acronyms?"

He shrugs. "Noted, and when I can, yes."

"It's really irritating to begin with," Rose offers, readjusting her hair to brush it back from her face. "But after a while, you get used to it. I don't even notice it anymore."

"And Rose here closes her eyes whenever someone else yawns in an attempt to stop herself from doing it... *yeah*" —he rolls his eyes in her direction— "we all noticed."

He looks triumphant in his declaration, crossing his arms over his chest in victory. "Joanie stares too long in an attempt to psych people out, for reasons yet to be determined. Tamra crosses her fingers as she sneezes, Vera complains consistently about her age, Quinn will never sit with her back toward the door and Rae pretends she's a vegetarian when she's very much a carnivore."

I blink.

"What I'm trying to tell you is that we're a collection of misfits. We're quirky, intense... but we've created a family of sorts."

I smile. "I don't like to be touched."

Clapping his hands together Dex hollers. "Meant to be, chicka. Welcome to our family."

I glance around the group, small smirks ticking their lips upward in varying stages of amusement. Ducking my head, I hide my own, a little embarrassed at how happy I feel at being welcomed into this eclectic group of people. I haven't felt this at peace in too long. It's nice.

"Now," Dex declares, louder than necessary. "Rules of Book Club."

"There are rules?"

He frowns. "Uh, yeah. We take this shit seriously."

"You're allowed to vote for a genre that's a no-go for you. We put it to the group, and if your vote reaches the majority, no one can select that genre come their month."

Seven very opposing stares settle on me.

"I have to pick now?"

"Yes," Joanie sighs.

"Sci-fi?" I test.

Rae claps. "Fuck. Yes. That's a tie, baby. Stranger game."

I look to Dex. "Rae voted to veto sci-fi donkeys ago, the vote was four to three. Your vote takes it to a tiebreak."

"Stranger game?" I question.

"First person that walks past our table, we ask them if they'd read sci-fi, whichever way they vote is the final say."

"Stops the arguments," Quinn offers. "Books can make people nasty."

"Excuse me." Vera stops a well-dressed male, suit fitted to his body like a glove. "Do you read sci-fi?"

His forehead creases in distaste. "No, I don't read. I prefer movies."

Tamra and Rose gag, falling into fits of giggles when he shifts in embarrassment.

"Thank you." Vera dismisses him with a wave of her hand.

"Bet you he doesn't know how to find a fucking clitoris either," Joanie grumbles.

"Sci-fi is out," Rae smiles. "Taylor, you and me... we're gonna be the best of friends."

FOUR

My body is shaking, my heart fluttering in my chest faster than it should be. A feeling of sickness burying deep in my stomach and settling there.

I should go home.

Should.

But I've made it this far. Literally ten steps from Caffeine Coma, and I can't bring myself to turn around. I'm on edge. Brittlely so. Ready to crack open, and I have *no* idea why. I woke up like this, no rhyme, no reason. It happens every so often, but today has gone from fragile to worse. Almost as though the universe has pinpointed me as its entertainment for the day, watching, waiting for me to shatter. Break open into a million and one indiscriminate pieces, too damaged to glue back together.

My fragility was envenomed by some random guy on the train, completely harmless by all outward standards, aside from the minor fact that he was standing *too* close. My personal space was pervaded, worse, I was trapped in that nightmare.

I'm not an idiot, I understand the risks of taking public transportation. That the overflowing capacity of bodies means we're packed in like sardines. But close wasn't even the right term, his body was pressed *heavily* against mine. Close alludes to cramped, he was *on*. I couldn't move. I'd shift, but another body would be *right* there, so I'd shuffle back into my usual safe zone. He'd apologize on a reluctant smile all the while all I could concentrate on was the thought that I was about a millisecond away from spraying him with the bile of my stomach.

Eyes closed, I found myself breathing; thick, measured inhales inflating my lungs. Only to push them back out with purpose through the pursed pinch of my lips. I fought so hard to remove myself from my surroundings, from the sensory overload suffocating me. Avoidance seemed safer than the alternative of having to actually *deal*, to cope with the harsh reality of me diving head first into a tailspin of hysteria.

Completely dissociated with my sense of self, I missed my stop. Searching for my way back into the present, I'm lost, scattered. Strewn across a multitude of versions of who I am.

Zoe Lincoln. *Victim.*

Taylor Smith. *Ghost.*

Truth is, I have no idea who I am.

I ran from the subway as soon as the doors opened, gulping for breath. Only to inhale *his* cologne. Again, that happens from time to time and I can move past it without freaking out like I am right now. But my already shaky and disoriented self almost fell to the ground in panic. In fact, I found the closest bench and dropped down, letting myself cry. I'm a mess. Or more, a greater mess than I usually am.

Which leads to now, about to step foot into Caffeine Coma ready to spontaneously combust.

Like I said, I should go home. But home is quiet. I'm alone, kept company by my disinterested cat and my own haunted thoughts and paranoia.

Reaching into my pocket, I grab hold of the carved chess queen, rubbing my thumb over the hard edges, along the soft line of the base. I breathe. Like Hannah reminded me. Triggers. Fucking everywhere. But like the talisman I chose, I'm fucking strong. The most powerful player in the story of my life. Not him. Not anyone else. *Me*.

"Yo, Taylor." Rake pops his head out of the door. "You okay? Look like you've seen a ghost."

I force a laugh, dropping the queen piece back into my jacket. "Something like that. I'm good."

I follow him inside considering he's one of the few males in the world I feel comfortable being around. He'd be in his mid-sixties. A long white Santaesque beard covering his chin, falling all the way to mid chest. His hair is the exact same color, likely the same length, always tied at the nape of his neck like a founding father. The tattoos up his arm are as colorful as the black shirts and cargo pants he only ever wears, shrouding him in darkness. But his eyes are kind, his nature more so. The moment I met him, he read my need for space, for less than zero *actual* human contact. He hired me to make coffee and lets me do my thing.

"Busy one today, Swifty."

The day I met Rake - which is his real name, I asked - I was met with silence on introduction, a head tilt added in for effect. "Like the singer?" he responded and from that single moment, that's the only name he's ever called me, even my name badge reads that way.

It's ridiculous, but it's Rake, and I like him, so I like it.

Moving into the break room, I search through my locker. Anti-anxiety meds have been a fixture in my life since the incident. In fact, to begin with, I was taking a cocktail of medication to help me keep calm, to lift me up when the grays and blacks of the world seemed as bleak as my outlook. Nowadays my cocktail isn't so full, but Valium remains a staple. Not all the time. Not every day, or even every week. But every so often, on a day like today, when my nerves feel electrified, and my heart is so tight in my chest I feel it ready to explode from the ribs scarcely big enough to keep it contained, I need an assist. Swallowing the small pill, I tip my head back, eyes closed to remember my breathing. I focus on my breath, on the pull of it through my core, centering me to the present.

Apron hung over my neck, I tie it around my waist, making my way to my station, greeting Mya with a silent wave. For the next two hours, I get lost in ground coffee. My voice, on autopilot, doesn't shake when I recite names for to-go orders. I avoid interaction with everyone with the exception of Rake and Mya.

Finishing off a soy latte, I slide it along the bench. "Soy latte for—" I glance up at the screen, my voice cutting off.

"Miller?" A young guy steps up, hand wrapped around the paper cup on a smile.

I stare at him blankly, the numbness I'd found over the last few hours dissipating like a cloud of smoke, exploding in my face in a timely reminder that he still controls the larger part of my psyche. The fear I seem intent on holding onto, greater than my strength.

I force a smile at the stranger, turning away before I can see his smile morph into confusion.

I focus on the short black cursor blinking at me from the screen by my work station.

Pulling my hair off my neck, I tie a band around it, pulling it into a high ponytail, needing air to touch the damp skin.

"Nice tattoo."

I glance up at the girl by the counter, my brows pulled together in confusion. "What?" I bite out, somewhat unceremoniously.

"The semicolon behind your ear." She looks *into* me, likely trying to convey something deeper, but I ignore it, not caring for her support.

"It's a birthmark," I lie, yanking at the tie to let my hair fall around my shoulders once again.

Her smile turns sad, a pity framing her face that fires my anger. "If you say so."

I make her coffee, ignoring her probing stare.

"One day you'll wear it without fear, without shame," she offers, grabbing hold of the coffee I slide toward her. "You'll realize it's a badge, one that definitively showcases you're a survivor. A warrior."

A semicolon stares up at me from her wrist, and my eyes travel upward to her face. "See you around, Swifty."

I pause, a smile creeping onto my lips. It's only then that I notice the audience she'd created, the line to the register watching on in interest.

The smile that had been forming on my face drops away with force, embarrassment shading my cheeks.

Ten minutes later, heartbeat still fluttering like a racehorse, the color having faded from my cheeks, I think about the girl.

A survivor.

A warrior.

I consider that she's right, more I *hope* she is.

"Tripp," I speak loudly. "Short black."

No one moves toward the glass, and I repeat his name.

Shrugging, I move on.

"Swifty," Rake calls out from the register. "Guy in the corner ordered that, tipped to have someone bring it over."

I glance at the glass, then back to Rake, and back again.

Rake doesn't spare me a second glance, already onto serving the next customer, and I retrieve the small inconspicuous coffee cursing *Tripp.*

The crowd within the coffee shop has died down significantly from this morning. But in our nonstop conveyor of serving customers and making coffee, the shop is a train wreck. Empty cups are discarded along stained tables, dirtied spoons leaving surfaces damp, crumbs of food scattered amongst the mess. A potent reminder that people are pigs.

Doubling-back to the counter, I grab a fresh cloth, tucking it into my apron strings on a muted string of cuss words directed at the general population. Weaving through tables, I move toward the smooth and smoky voice echoing quietly from the far corner of the space. Phone attached to his ear, the stranger doesn't notice my approach and I'm grateful that he won't attempt to *chat.* Legs splayed, his elbows rest upon his knees, head tipped down as he speaks. The indiscriminate color of his brown hair is being gripped by his large hand, frustration clear in the white-knuckled hold. Paperwork adorns the table in front of him chaotically, his laptop open on top, the screen pushed down to hide the contents. I place his coffee down in the sliver of space I see amongst his mess, turning away before he can look up.

Stacking cups on the table beside him, I wipe along the scratched and stained surface, clearing it. I scrape at the chocolate crumbs encrusted on the wood, working to remove the remnants of someone's morning tea with a frown.

Straightening, I tuck my cloth in my apron once again, picking up the mess. It happens so quick, I've barely registered what actually happened before my cheeks are red with embarrassment and I'm apologizing profusely.

His hand is big, powerful, seizing my wrist with purpose. My whole body startles, the cups in my hand flying forward without intention. Coffee dregs fly over his white shirt, falling along his canvas sneakers in a milky rain.

Hand flying from my skin, I watch them lift in surrender.

"I'm so sorry," he apologizes sotto voce. "I didn't mean to frighten you."

I swallow the bile rushing up my throat, the shock of his touch lacerating through my body like Morse code.

"You shouldn't just grab someone like that," I scold, the tremor in my voice both obvious and embarrassing.

"Totally agree. I just wanted to say thank you, for bringing my coffee." He gestures at his table, stepping back cautiously. More for me and my scattered brain than for his own safety.

I feel like a fool. It wasn't even the fact that he had actually *touched* me. Which is surprising in itself and definitely something I know Hannah would deem as important. I think more of the shock of it happening without my knowledge was what caused my irrational reaction. The unexpected nature of it.

"I'm *so* sorry," I duck my eyes. "I've thrown coffee all over your shirt and shoes. I'm an idiot."

He shakes his head. "Someone grabbed me without me seeing it coming, I'd likely react the same way," he lies.

"You wouldn't," I combat with a roll of my eyes. "But I appreciate you trying to make me feel better. I really am sorry. You've caught me on an off day."

Lie. One he likely can see shaded along my cheeks, but he doesn't comment.

I drop down, collecting the cups I'd so ungraciously thrown at him. He follows my movements, helping.

"Stop." I push his hand out of the way. "Just... I don't know... complain to Rake about me throwing coffee at you or go back to whatever you were working on. Drop your PayPal or Venmo details at the counter and I'll send you the cash to replace your clothes."

He continues cleaning without pause, irritating me further. I stop, staring at the top of his head.

Noticing my hands have stopped moving, he glances up. "What?"

His eyes are blue. Actually, more a silver. That awkward shade in between where some days they look grey, others more definitively blue. If you were to ask him, he'd likely tell you the shade changes depending on what he wears or his mood. Eyebrows sit heavily over his imperfect blue eyes, thick and similarly colored to his thick and disheveled hair. A straight nose, perfectly aligned to his face flares intermittently in time with a silent sniff. A scatter of hair decorates the bottom half of his face, complementing the relaxed attire covering his body.

"I'm Tripp," he offers.

"I know."

I move back to cleaning, taking the cups he had retrieved for me from his hand, careful not to touch him.

"Swifty," he tests. "Is that your real name?"

His voice lacks the twang of a native New Yorker and I'm intrigued to find I quite like the sound of it. Quiet without being soft. Husky without the hint of a mumble, the sound clear and concise.

"The only name you need to know," I answer, standing. "Again, I'm sorry for ruining your clothes. I insist you let me replace them."

He waves me off. "Not necessary, Swifty," he tests the name on a frown, not comfortable with the sound of it along his tongue. "This white shirt was old anyway." We both glance down, zipping up his hoodie, he shrugs. "All fixed, and I'll throw my shoes in the washer. It'll be like it never happened."

I consider him for a beat before nodding. "If you're sure."

I walk away before he can speak to me further.

"Everything okay?" Rake questions as I move back behind the counter.

Dropping the empty cups into the trash, I shake my head. "I just threw coffee all over the guy that tipped well. Are you gonna fire me?" I turn to him, waiting for him to respond.

"He didn't seem to find an issue with it, why should I?" His eyebrows pull together.

I shrug. "Maybe he'll never come back, and you'll lose his business. Maybe he'll one star your shop on Facebook or something."

"Never seen him before, so he's of no loss to me if he doesn't come back. In saying that, you've been off all day...

Are you sure you're okay? It's quiet now, I'd have no problem if you wanted to take the rest of the day off."

Checking my watch, I nod. "Yeah, maybe I will. Go for a run, clear my head," I offer unnecessarily.

"I think that sounds like a good idea. We'll see you on Wednesday."

Pulling at the strings of my apron, I offer Rake a grateful smile. "Thanks, Rake."

He only winks in response, moving away to serve another customer.

My lungs burn with the need to pull in a bigger breath. I push harder, inhaling heavily through my nose. The loud slap of my shoes echoes with every moment they connect with the treadmill. Lifting only to hit down again. Over and over. Faster. A sheen of sweat sticks to my skin and I lift my towel, rubbing the drops from my forehead. The woman next to me jumps, feet landing on the stationary sides, the belt continuing at an alarming speed as she sucks down a large gulp of water. I can hear her music, the thick rhythm filtering between us even though she's wearing headphones. Water bottle tucked away, she jumps back onto the speeding belt without missing a beat, her feet continuing like she'd never taken a break.

Jesus.

As convenient as it would be to take a drink of water without hitting the stop button, I'd fall ass over fucking tits trying to do something like that, I have zero doubt.

Hello humiliation, welcome home.

No thanks, I'll stay here in my hole of comfort, content and more importantly, *cautious* in my clumsiness.

I already feel better. The anxious fire of my day easing with every labored breath I take. It happens from time to time. The panic. It occurs less and less as more time passes. Still, it always catches me unaware. Which randomly is the thing that throws me most. It's ridiculous. My body and mind react as though I've never experienced the panic before. It's moments like today that fuel the uselessness I feel in my own skin. It's a horrible sense of self. Incompetence. Running lets me clear my head enough to let me claim my mind back. It helps to erase the thoughts that storm black and gray in my mind, promising me it'll always be this way. Exhausting my body physically kills their momentum, and I get to see the thoughts for what they are. Lies. Pushed into my conscience with the sole purpose of self-sabotage.

FIVE

I close the paperback with force, throwing it onto my couch in irritation. I glance at the Netflix inspired cover, the eerie stare of the male lead boring into mine causing me to frown once again. Leaning forward I retrieve my laptop, logging onto Amazon, nail caught between my teeth. I read through review after review, my frown deepening with every word.

Praise for the protagonist.

Irritation and hate thrown at the heroine.

Opening the message app on my Mac, I search for Rae's name.

Taylor: What in the ever-loving did I just read?

My eyes fall along the paperback once again, and I scowl at it.

Rae: Fabulous, no?

Taylor: I'd say creepy... Have you read the reviews? People are twisted.

Rae: Ha! That's the brilliance of this story though. You have a sick son-of-a-bitch, a seriously twisted motherfucker... but the audience *empathizes* with him... to a point... He's intriguing. His internal monologue so warped and, I don't know... charming?

Taylor: The world has romanticized a predator.

Rae: Yes. Forget the current climate we live in tho. Just consider the brilliance of the author. She took someone we should be afraid of and made him, by all outward appearances... *approachable*. A guy you would date.

Taylor: If the guy were unattractive and socially awkward, readers wouldn't be glamorizing him.

Rae: Exactly. Not all predators are hideous and strange, T.

I pause, staring at the words of her text.

Not all predators are hideous.

I know this first-hand. My predator was, at first impression, not just handsome. He was *beautiful*.

Cut jawline. Exaggerated lips. Tall. Broad. *Beautiful.*

Cheekbones carved like stone, tapered all the way down to a strong jaw. His smile was *show-stopping,* a gesture that took over his entire face, making you feel an overwhelming sense of pleasure. Thick, dark brows hung heavily over his deep chocolate colored eyes. He was tall without being towering. Broad without being stocky. Perfection. Beautiful... to look at anyway.

It was his eyes that gave him away, the moment they met mine head on. They set me on edge immediately. The way he looked *into* me. With a simple glance, I felt a flame of unease ignite deep in my gut, and as the night passed it only raged further. He leered without actually staring. I felt dirty well before his hands touched my skin without permission.

My predator was pure, irredeemable evil wrapped in pretty packaging. Which made him a level of dangerous women weren't used to seeing.

Taylor: You're right. The author has weaved the most frightening villain into the story disguised as the hero we long for.

Rae: Bingo. I can't wait to fucking dissect everyone's thoughts on this at book club.

I get ready for work in a book haze, my thoughts completely derailed by the fictional bookstore manager and his quiet appeal to readers. Rae's thought process intrigued me, it *challenged* me. Something I haven't let myself feel, with the exception to my sessions with Hannah of course, in a really long time.

The café is quiet when I step through the door, and I don't know whether to be pleased or disappointed. The quiet lets me run away with my thoughts, and where I'm at right now, I can't be certain on whether that's a good thing or not.

"The guy you painted with coffee is back," Rake greets me, gesturing toward the corner of the shop. "Told you we had nothing to worry about."

I glance toward the direction Rake points, but he's hidden behind the large chair he's lounged upon. I see his foot though, his black Converse high-top peeking from the side of the chair.

"Has he ordered?"

"Hmm?" Rake looks over at me. "No. Only walked in about two minutes before you did."

Tying my apron strings, I nod, moving to my station.

Short black in hand, I stare at the corner of the shop, my hand shaking slightly.

"He's not gonna bite, Swifty."

I swallow down my nerves, glancing at Rake on a stiff nod.

This is so out of character for me. *Interaction.* Normal human interaction. Hannah is on me about it all the time.

I can do this. I threw coffee at the poor guy. Then threw attitude because he caught me by surprise. Least I can do is buy him a coffee in apology considering he won't let me replace the clothes I ruined.

Steeling my spine, I move toward where he's sitting, kind of hoping he's on the phone again and I don't need to actually speak. At least then I tried.

Kind of.

Unfortunately for me, he's bent over endless sheets of

paper, a crease in his brow so prominent it actually hurts to look at.

Moving around his table, I place his coffee down and he looks up immediately.

"Swifty." He sounds so pleased to see me, genuine happiness replacing the intense concentration he was moments ago stuck in.

A small grin tickles the edge of my mouth, but I stop it forming further. "It's Taylor. Rake, the owner," I clarify, "thinks he's funny."

He frowns. "I don't get it."

Picking at the sleeves of my shirt, I shift uncomfortably. "Taylor Swift?" I test. "The pop star."

Bottom lip tipped out, his head shakes side-to-side.

I pause my fidgeting. "You've never heard of Taylor Swift? You never saw Kanye jump on stage and humiliate her with the whole 'Beyoncé had one of the best albums of all time.'"

Strong lines from along his unshaven cheeks, a smirk twitching at his lips. "That was an exceptional Kanye impression," he praises, and a laugh barks from my mouth before I'm able to stop it.

"Of course, I know who Taylor Swift is. I just like that you're talking to me instead of throwing coffee."

My cheeks shade. "About that," I start, clearing my throat. "I was completely out of sorts that day, in truth, I'm out of sorts most days, but that day I was particularly inept at life. I'm sorry for throwing stale coffee at you, and for then acting like it was your fault."

He waves me off. "Taylor," he tests my name along his tongue. "You have nothing to apologize for. I told you that. Look" —he kicks his foot out— "like brand new."

My gaze falls to his sneaker and I nod. "Still, you won't let me pay to replace your shirt, the least I could do was buy you a coffee."

He glances at the table, placing his pen down to give me his undivided attention. "Does that mean you'll join me?"

I swallow the shock of his invitation. "Oh. Umm... I'm working. I... No. I..."

"Taylor," he stops my rambling. "It's fine. I was kidding. Well, not really, but it's fine. You're forgiven. Thank you for the coffee."

I watch him for a beat, my eyes scanning his face openly. He leaves me to my quiet perusal, and forcing a smile, I walk off.

"It was nice to meet you, Taylor."

I glance over my shoulder. His body is twisted around his chair, his gaze on me. Biting my bottom lip, I hide my uncertainty.

I'm hyper-aware of his presence in the shop. Which is crazy because he keeps to himself. He speaks quietly, his hushed tone only heard when the space is completely quiet. He doesn't move. He drinks his coffee and he works.

Rake moves toward him and without conscious thought, I stop mid-way through making a coffee, watching them. They interact easy enough and a thorn of jealousy stabs at my side. There are times when I wish I wasn't so awkward, so uncomfortable in myself.

Truth be told, I can't even determinately pinpoint *why* I am the way I am. Sure, I've been through a trauma. But it was a specific trauma. An incident involving one single human being. My hesitation to interact with the remaining population of the world floors me. I know that not everyone

I come into contact with is a rapist. I know very few of the billions of people who make up the world are violent. Yet, I keep myself at a distance, afraid of my own fucking shadow.

Hannah and I have spoken about this more times than I'd be comfortable in admitting. She calls them intrusive thoughts. Threatening and unwanted thoughts that creep into my mind, and refuse to leave. She tells me my anxiety is what gives them power.

"Tripp wants another coffee, sweetheart."

Rake's baritone pulls me from the prison of my mind, and I nod. "Sure."

He doesn't ask, but I know he wants me to deliver it to Tripp's table.

"Will you sit?" Tripp asks as I bend to place his coffee carefully amidst his paperwork.

"I told you, I'm working," I argue.

He considers me for a moment. "Rake told me you were due for a break."

I swallow my animosity, glancing at Rake in irritation.

"I don't like decisions being made about me without my involvement." I focus back on his contemplative stare.

"No decision made without you, Taylor. I won't be offended if you say no. Rake only noted that you tend to work through all your breaks."

I roll my shoulders considering my options. Walking away without a word, I move behind the counter, untying my apron before I can second guess myself. Pulling a bottle of water from the fridge, I move toward Tripp again, pausing only to start forward once more.

He smiles when I sit down across from him, a pleasant

surprise letting him drop his pen and shift forward on his chair.

"We've not officially met," he holds his hand out. "I'm Tripp Tanner."

I glance to his hand, blinking.

Honesty Hannah's voice echoes in my head.

"I'm not comfortable touching people I don't know," I murmur.

I expect him to frown, to look at me with regret that he invited me to sit down. Instead, he nods his head in easy acceptance. "Fair enough."

"Taylor Smith," I introduce myself, and for the first time in a long while, I feel guilty about lying.

Tripp seems like a genuine person. He's kind, or more his eyes seem kind. With the way he looks at me, I half expect him to reject my name, to call me out on my mistruth. Of course, he doesn't.

"Well, it's nice to officially meet you, Taylor Smith."

I take a sip of water. "You said that already," I argue, twisting the cap back onto my bottle.

"I did," he laughs. "But this is *official*."

I nod in agreement. "It's nice to meet you."

Retrieving his coffee, he looks at the water bottle held tightly in my hand, my nerves showing with the way I rip at the label. "You don't drink coffee?"

Clearing my throat, I place my bottle by my feet, working to stop my hands from fidgeting. "Yeah, I do. When I work, I smell it constantly. Those days I never seem to have a craving for it."

"What are you working on?" I shift the conversation to him, and he glances at his paperwork.

"A case. I'm a lawyer."

Glancing at his attire, the causal grey shirt stretched across his chest, dark wash jeans pulled tightly against his thighs. I raise an eyebrow. "You don't look like a lawyer."

He grins, and I reciprocate.

Tripp looks good when he smiles, or so I've observed. More handsome than usual. A twinkle glistening in his perfectly imperfect colored eyes. I've counted two different types of smiles so far. A closed lipped pull of his mouth, and a full-fledged grin. The open smile tends to occur in line with a laugh, a full show of his straight, white teeth, lips stretching to a point their color lightens. His closed one, the one he offers most often is more a genuine pull of happiness, a gesture he can't control.

"I don't work full time within my business, I do a lot of pro-bono work. When I'm working on the pro-bono cases, I like to be away from my desk, *when I can,*" he clarifies. "Suits are constrictive."

"You look too young to be half-retired."

He laughs. The full-fledged grin. The sound of his laughter dies off and he leans back in his chair, resting his foot over his knee. "I wouldn't exactly say that," he affirms. "Family business. For the moment my father is still very active at work, it gives me the opportunity to do work *I'm* passionate about."

I look down, shocked by his openness.

"Also, I'm not *that* young." He winks.

"How old?" I ask before I can stop myself. "I'm sorry. That was rude."

"Not at all, I'm thirty-six. You?"

"Thirty-one," I answer before I can consider that I've just answered a personal question without freaking out.

"What do you do with yourself when you're not here?" he carries on, unaware of my internal dilemma.

"I work from home," I offer. "I picked up this job to get out of the house, it's easy to sit in your comfort zone and never leave. Peopling isn't something I do overly well, this job was my way to challenge myself."

"I like that," he murmurs. "What do you do for work?"

Settling back into my own seat, I retrieve my water, unscrewing the cap. "I'm an illustrator."

His eyes widen at that, and I smile. "That's cool," he compliments.

I nod. "Yeah, I used to work in graphic design, but drawing is where my passion lies. A few years ago I changed a few things in my life, my career was one of them. I'm happy with what I do now. I work my own hours, doing what I love."

"Sounds like a good life."

I blink.

Sounds like a good life.

Is it?

A good life? Mine?

I consider that my work is definitely a *good* part of my life.

"Yeah," I agree. "I guess you're right. What pro-bono work do you do?" I take a sip of water, watching him.

"I do work a little in line with the innocent project," he tests.

I sit up straight. "You work to have people convicted of crimes released?"

The clear change in my tone is obvious, cutting between us like a knife's edge.

"*Innocent* people," he clarifies. "Yes."

"How do you *know* they're innocent?" I argue, my voice rising.

"I review their files," he remains composed, his voice never wavering. "I see reasonable doubt."

"Reasonable doubt," I test, the words like acid burning my tongue.

"Yes," he answers confidently. "Reasonable doubt."

"What if they're guilty?" I whisper.

He leans forward, eyes focused intently on mine. "What if they're innocent?"

I consider his point.

"It's an age-old argument, Taylor. Would you prefer a guilty man go free, or an innocent man spend his life in prison for a crime he didn't commit?"

I move to speak, my answer catching in my throat.

"Exactly," he sits back. "Our judicial system was constructed to ensure anyone locked away was done so through the *highest* burden of proof. Sometimes it's wrongly applied."

"And sometimes people who deserve to rot in jail, walk away." My voice wavers and I hate that he saw my vulnerability, open and available for him to dissect.

He nods. "True. I work to rectify some of the wrongful sentences handed down."

"Why?" I ask rudely. "There must be a reason, a defining moment that pushed you toward this."

His gaze falls over me, the stiffness in my posture, the

tightness of anger in my jaw. "Why not? People are wrongly accused *all* the time."

"But if you weren't *there*, how do you know that?"

He scratches the back of his neck awkwardly. His phone rings and I take the opportunity to leave. "I'll let you get that."

Sighing, he picks up his cell, sliding his finger across the screen. "Tanner."

SIX

Tripp Tanner has come into Caffeine Coma twice weekly for the last month and I've spoken to him a grand total of zero times. He's given me the space I've silently requested. He orders his coffee, smiles his thanks when I hand it over but doesn't attempt conversation and no longer requests I bring it over to him. For a split second, I thought there was a possibility that he was irritated with me, but his smiles are still as warm as they were when we first met. It's obvious he's leaving the ball in my court. Letting me make the decision as to whether I care to speak to him again. His career is what it is, should I want to know him, we're both very much aware of the fact that I'll need to come to terms with where his passion lies.

"Why are you avoiding him?"

I consider Hannah's question, picking up a disgruntled Potter to look at his face in distraction.

"I don't know," I lie.

Hannah sees through it though, waiting quietly for me to reconsider my avoidance.

Letting my cat jump from my hands, I sigh loudly. "I guess the thought of him supporting people that don't deserve it, people like Miller, struck a nerve."

"Before your attack, had you met Tripp, what would you have thought of his career?"

I try to recall a time when my thoughts weren't tainted by my life experience.

"Maybe admirable?" I question my own statement, and Hannah, again waits for me to continue, letting me work through my own thoughts.

"I see the positive in what he does," I implore, speaking the truth. "*But,*" I combat. "I also can't move past the fact that he could work to free a predator, someone violent, someone who *should* be paying for their choices."

"Considering your past, it's not unreasonable for you to react the way you did. But to be brutally honest, you're projecting. You're taking your negative experience and pushing it onto something you'd once upon a time find noble. From what you've told me, he doesn't appear perturbed by your reaction, more understanding?"

I consider Tripp and his behavior over the past few weeks. His interaction with me, however small, shows no animosity. In fact, he's cautiously considerate, respecting my need to process, my need for space.

Hannah takes my silence as an affirmation, continuing after a beat. "I'm most intrigued at your want to engage with this man. Zoe, this is a massive step."

I shift uncomfortably. "I think you're reading into it," I argue meekly.

"No. A few months ago there is *no* way you would have

voluntarily sat down with a man and engaged in open conversation. He makes you feel comfortable, *safe* in a way."

"Is that weird?" I lean forward, needing her educated reasoning on the stranger that has side-tracked my thoughts.

She sighs. "Zoe. Our aim with these sessions is to move you back into a life that you want. Friendships, *relationships,* purpose, *sex.* You're climbing obstacles each and every day, you're looking at the mountains of your anxiety and you're scaling them. You're still speaking with Rae regularly?"

Her memory is ridiculous. I offer a small detail, and she holds that insignificant tidbit, ready to fire it as ammunition to neutralize the roadblocks that I, myself, raise when pushed out of my comfort zone.

"Yeah," I answer. "Just via text, but she's asked me to breakfast this Sunday."

"Perfect." Hannah's hands open in praise before clapping back together. "It's not unfathomable that a man is piquing your interest. It was going to happen at some point."

"We've spoken a grand total of two times, one of which I threw coffee on him. I'd hardly say he's interested. Just kind."

Hannah laughs. "I don't know many men who would continue a conversation with a woman they weren't interested in after being doused in stale coffee. His motive aside, be it romantic or not, how do you feel?"

"He's handsome." I drop my eyes, massaging my palm. "He's easy to talk to, from the snippets we've shared. There's a... *pull,* a magnetism about him."

"Talk to him," she implores.

Palms running along my face, I groan. "Let's say I do talk to him. Let's say things progress, and by some miracle he *is* interested... I don't know how to navigate a relationship."

"I disagree," she counters. "You held healthy relationships prior to Miller, and you'll have them after. Your experience is definitely going to shape the way you approach a relationship post your attack, but honesty is key. Things progress, you explain to him that you have limitations and that it will move slowly. If he's invested, he'll understand."

"I can't lead with what happened."

Her eyes close. "Of course not." She opens them again. "But you can tell him that your preference is a pace likely slower than he's used to. Explain you have limits at this stage. He's smart, he'll read your cues. Zoe, you don't need to lie, but you can share the truths you're willing to. If he dives into something you're not comfortable talking about, *tell him.*"

"I'm scared," I blurt out loudly.

"And that's okay. It doesn't mean you should hide away from the potential of something good, *great* even. You deserve happiness, Zoe. Don't shy away from it out of fear."

I let silence drift around us.

"Will you talk to him again?" She breaks the quiet with her whispered question, and I swallow, looking up at her.

"Maybe."

Tripp is in his usual seat days later, laptop rested atop of his knees, eyes trained on his screen. The furrow in his brow is back, the deep line of concentration that makes him look more severe, more imposing. Cleaning the table three over from him, I stare unabashedly. Too caught up in his work, he doesn't notice, so I continue.

Nearing forty, he's still holding on to the easiness of his youth while comfortably creeping up to his middle-aged years. Tripp Tanner has aged well. Sure, his face sports a few lines along the corners of his eyes, and faint lines bracket his mouth, a side-effect of smiling often. Lines that women pay money to smooth out, he wears like a badge of honor, and he does it *well*.

Jacket discarded on the chair beside him, his tan arms show strong definition each and every time he moves. A small flex here as he rolls his shoulders. A pulsation of veins as he clenches his fist to relieve his RSI from typing. A tattoo peeks from the cuff of his shirt and I take a step closer, working to see the small flock of birds scattered along his skin. They stop mid-way down the underside of his forearm; intricate birds in differing stages of wingspan. His left hand bears no wedding ring, his fingers are long, strong, with distinct veins extending from his knuckles past his wrist.

Rubbing his eyes, he yawns, stretching his neck this way and that.

He even looks good yawning. How that's possible, I have no clue, but Tripp Tanner makes it work. The way his big hand loosely wraps around his face, covering both his nose and mouth, eyes closing. A small shout trails the end of his yawn, hand closing into a fist before pulling away, his now open eyes drifting across the café.

The unusual shade of his eyes catches my stare and I look

away fast, re-wiping the table I'd spent the last ten minutes cleaning.

Confident, I've given myself enough time to recover from being caught, I glance up from behind my lashes. While kind enough to have turned away leaving me to my mortification, a small smile still tickles at the corner of his lips and I inwardly curse and admire his gentle consideration.

Standing to full height, I inhale heavily. He lets me approach without audience, waiting until I'm standing directly in front of him before lifting his head to greet me.

"May I sit?" I ask, quiet hesitation in my tone.

"Please." He gestures to the seat in front of his, closing his laptop to offer his undivided attention.

"I'm an awkward human," I offer by way of apology.

"All the most interesting people are."

I smile a small smile, cheeks warming in embarrassment.

"For personal reasons... your career brought up some.... *stuff* and I reacted... *poorly*."

He leans forward on his chair, sliding his laptop onto the table. "Not at all. Taylor, your honest reaction isn't something to apologize for. Trust me when I tell you that your response was tame in comparison to others I've experienced. You don't have to agree with what I do for us to be... *friends?*"

"You're not a true New Yorker," I observe, steering the conversation away from the awkward and unnecessary topic of our relationship.

"True," he concurs. "From all around actually. My mom and dad separated when I was young. Dad's been in New York for most of my life, but Mom moved around a lot. My time with them was shared. I've spent a few years working in London recently as well."

"Siblings?"

He shakes his head. "Only child."

"Same as me."

"What about you?" His eyes catalog my face, blinking over my features in curiosity.

Readjusting my apron at my knees, I clear my throat. "From near Charlottesville," I offer. "Moved here a few years ago for a change of scenery."

His gaze skates over the soft brown strands of my hair that have managed to escape my ponytail. "I've spent some time in Charlottesville." His eyes fall to mine then, his soft, closed-lipped smile shining at me in appreciation.

"You have green eyes," he observes randomly.

"Yours are an odd shade of blue, sometimes gray. Maybe more steel?"

His quiet smile morphs into a wider grin, a brief flash of his teeth showing. He liked that I noticed. That I looked hard enough to file something about him in my conscious purposefully.

"What do you do for fun, Taylor?"

Could he have asked a more awkward question?

Avoid human contact.

Pretend to be someone else.

"I read," I offer instead. "I actually just joined a book club. I moved out here alone. I haven't had a lot of opportunities to meet people, *friends,*" I clarify. "Like I said, I'm more than a little graceless. Meeting new people, sharing things about who I am makes me want to break out in hives." My honesty shocks me, but not enough to stop me from talking. "I'm a homebody, and am happy enough getting caught up in work, and spending time with my cat, Potter."

"Like Harry Potter?"

I chuckle. "Yeah. I'm a total Harry nerd."

"I've never read the books, or watched the movies for that matter."

My jaw drops. "What? How is that even possible?"

He laughs on a gentle lift of his shoulders. "Life has been busy, up until recently I've worked big hours, watching movies wasn't really a high priority."

My eyes narrow teasingly. "Fair enough... So when you're not having coffee thrown at you in your regular coffee haunt, what do you do with yourself?"

"You'll think I'm lame."

I can't contain the laugh that escapes me loudly. "I literally just finished telling you I watch Harry Potter with my cat."

The full-fledged grin. A small bark of laughter.

"I play fantasy baseball."

I blink.

"You think I'm lame," he chuckles at my silence.

"No," I bite out. "I just, I thought that was a made up thing only mentioned in movies."

His laughter rings out around the cafe so loud, heads turn our way. It's a thick laugh, full of happiness, rough in the scratch of his throat.

"So we're both nerds," I declare as his laughter tapers off.

"Both nerds," he agrees.

We spend the next twenty minutes lost in conversation, Tripp attempting to explain how fantasy baseball works and failing. Miserably. He takes it in stride though, refusing to give up hope that I'll get it eventually.

"I should get back to work," I murmur as our conversation tapers off.

Nodding regretfully, he lets his gaze drift across my face. "I enjoyed this."

Standing, I smile. "Me too."

"I'll see you soon, Taylor."

I feel like the worst kind of fraud. A liar. A phony. Truth is, as hard as I work to identify as *Taylor,* there's a massive disconnect. Hannah likes to think it's me, the *Zoe* me, fighting through the façade I've built to cope with my grief.

I take a step away, turning back. "My friends call me Zee."

He arches a dark brow.

"A story I'm not ready to share."

He accepts my explanation without issue. "Enjoy the rest of your day, Zee."

I don't read into how relaxed I feel at him using my *actual* name. My past creeping through the cracks in my soul, *with my permission.*

Lifting my hand, I wave, moving away and ignoring the probing stare from Rake as I shift back behind the coffee machine.

"Shift finished ten minutes ago, Swifty."

I glance at my watch. "Oh, I'm sorry Rake. I'm happy to work over, make up for the time I was caught up."

He smiles. "Honey, you never take a break, was nice to see. Go home. Enjoy your night."

SEVEN

"Day off?"

He moves his eyes from the hardcover in his hands, face warm and open at my approach.

"Sundays are sacred," he declares on a wink. "I'm here most Sundays, I've never seen you work this shift before."

I glance down at the apron in my hands. "Mya couldn't work her morning shift. Rake asked me to help cover the mid-morning crowd." I move to walk away. "Need a top off?"

He shakes his head. "I'm good, dove."

Dove. Not Taylor. Not even Zee. *Dove.*

I blink. Widely. Shocked and pleased all at once at the endearment. I force my feet forward, shuffling along the linoleum floor both confused and elated at how he makes me feel.

"Zee," he calls out, and I pause, twisting my entire body to look at him.

"You didn't ask me what I'm reading."

A cautious smile spreads across my face. "What are you reading, Tripp?"

Lifting his book, his eyes peek over the *Harry Potter and the Prisoner of Azkaban* cover and I can't stop the giggle that drifts between us.

"Please tell me you've read the first two before you started on book three."

Holding his place with a finger, he closes the book, resting it on his lap. "I have."

Bottom lip tipped out, my eyebrows rise in shock. "I'm impressed."

There's something about a man reading. A paperback held tightly in his hands, focus set solely on the world at his fingertips. He knows how to dream, to imagine the impossible, it's attractive beyond belief.

"Was wondering if you wanted to join my book club?" he continues.

"You're in a book club?" I ask skeptically.

His head tips to the side in consideration. "I mean, currently it's just me in the group, but I'm looking for another person to join if you're interested. Our first meeting is today at... when do you finish your shift?"

I laugh. "Lunchtime."

"Our first meeting starts at lunchtime today. Wait" —he holds up a hand— "have you read the first three Harry Potter books?" A dark brow lifts in challenge. "It's what we're discussing today."

"You know," I smirk, "I think I have."

"Well then, of course, you're welcome to join, I appreciate you asking. I look forward to it."

I turn away on a shake of my head, moving in the direction of the counter.

"Everything okay?" Rake queries. "You're smiling, but your forehead is all creased in confusion."

"Huh?" I glance up. "Yeah, I'm good," I dismiss his concern, pulling my apron over my head.

"Halloween is approaching, ready for the influx of pumpkin spice?" he jokes and my face twists in distaste.

"I still haven't forgiven you for conceding to the masses. That shit is nasty," I complain.

"It ain't that bad, Swifty."

I look to him in shock and he laughs heartily. "You're right, it's fucking disgusting. But it's business. The consumer gets what the consumer wants."

"If the leadup to Halloween wasn't so goddamn long, I'd take the month off in protest."

That earns me another thick barrel of laughter. "You couldn't leave me for that amount of time. Who would save me from Mya's recap of *The Bachelor?*"

I smile to myself, my hands busy with warming milk. "And here I thought you kept me around because I'm exceptional at my job."

"That too." He bumps my shoulder softly as he passes. "Thanks for covering today, I owe you one."

I stare at him a second. "You owe me nothing, Rake. I'm indebted to you for giving me this job."

His rough face warms at my words. "Let's call it even then."

I nod, words not necessary.

Rake knows he took a chance on me. I could barely speak when I walked into his shop asking for a job. I certainly didn't have a clue on how to make a decent cup of coffee. He wasn't deterred by my awkward fumbling or lack of experience though. He took one look into my eyes and hired me on the spot. Maybe it was out of pity, to begin with anyway, but we've established a friendship of sorts. He's one of the few people that understands I don't like talking about myself, or maybe he's just more accepting of my preference not to share. He never pries, never pushes our conversation further than I'm comfortable in going. He gets me, and I love the hell out of him for that.

"Thanks for helping this morning, sweetheart. Mya should be here in the next half an hour, why don't you finish up."

Wiping the counter, I nod without looking up. "Sure. Just going to make Tripp and I a drink."

I ignore the pause in his movements, the jolt of surprise in his person.

"Why don't you go sit down, I'll make them, bring them over."

I shake my head. "It's okay. I know how he takes it."

I ignore the probing stare boring into my profile, focusing on the task at hand, Tripp's short black.

Phone in hand, Tripp locks it as soon as I approach, sliding it into his pocket to offer me his full attention.

"Thank you." He takes the coffee I offer him.

"Finished your book?" I take a seat opposite him, taking a sip of my iced coffee.

"No milk. Hardcore," he teases. "Yes, I finished, can't you see my tears."

I sit silently, suddenly unsure of myself and my motivation for taking Tripp up on his offer.

Is this a date? A precursor of one? More importantly, is that what I'm hoping it to be?

"Do you believe in magic, dove?" He drops his voice, the soft whisper of his words captivating my attention in its entirety and cutting off my self-doubt without effort.

He called me it again. *Dove.* I consider questioning him on it, but refrain, too scared of what he'll say.

"I wish it were real," I answer truthfully. "The world of make-believe. The impossible. The extraordinary. Imagine that?" My voice has risen in its excitement, flashes of hope and wonder spiking my words in joy.

His face lifts at my reaction, the lines in his face buried deep with the wide smile that graces his lips.

"Do you?" I question him. "Believe in magic."

Taking a sip of coffee, he watches me over the rim of his cup. He takes his time answering, contemplating his words before letting them free.

"You'll think I'm lame," he smirks, placing his cup on the table beside his book.

His hands are big. Not obscenely so, just the right size to scream power and masculinity. The kind of hands that would feel calloused to the touch because he's not afraid of physical work, the kind that would feel both rough and gentle along your skin, the tender torment of passion behind his touch.

"No, I won't," I argue, annoyed that he seems to think so little of me and my opinion of him.

"I *do* believe in magic," he confesses, head tilted to the side, his gaze constantly roaming my face. "But not in the way you read it in a book." He gestures to the hardcover closed over by his coffee. "I see magic in life. I think the smell of rain and the feel of sunshine on your skin is magic. I believe that the sound of laughter and the taste of drying someone's tears is magic. Discovering new friends." He grins over at me. "Falling in *love,* first kisses, the taste of coffee, hearing your new favorite song for the first time, books, movies..." He trails off on a happy sigh, leaning forward to ensure we're not so far apart. "The world is full of magic, Zee. You don't even need to look hard to find it."

I stare at him blankly.

"You don't need sorting hats or wands or enchanted castles, you just gotta open your eyes, dove. The magic you're searching for, it's fucking surrounding you, *begging* you to see it."

Words fail me. I attempt to speak, multiple times. But fail, my mouth opening only to close again.

"Seeing someone for the first time," he whispers. "That second your eyes find them and your heart races in your chest." He stares right at me, the intensity of his eyes pinned on mine. "The moment when the world drops away and you'd give anything for them to *see* you, to talk to you... That right there" —he leans closer, his teeth dragging across his lips for a beat of time— "it's *all* magic. Best part, nothing make-believe about it. It's all fucking real."

My eyes burn. The sting of tears forcing me to blink.

"I envy your outlook," I scratch out, swallowing the razors in my throat.

"If you'd stop shying away from the world, you'd see that it sees *you* that way. You're exquisite, Zee. I almost think you're make believe."

I laugh then, a blush crawling up my neck so hot I could swear he could see flames. "Hardly. Me and my life are far from charmed. I'm a ghost, Tripp. I like it that way."

His eyes scrutinize me for longer than I'm comfortable. I shift in my seat. Coughing, I clear my throat, waiting for him to say something.

"I don't believe that," he finally speaks, a gentle reserve to his voice. "I think that you're in pain, and because of that, you're turning your back on the beauty the world has to offer. But even hiding, you're the loudest thing I've ever seen. I can't seem to ignore you, dove. Not that I care to try," he finishes softly.

I can't breathe. The intensity of his words like a choke hold, wrapped around my neck, strangling me in their beauty. The ivory touch of my skin heats, no doubt blossoming with a shade of pink, embarrassment once again changing my complexion. I duck my head, working to control the blush highlighting my face. The dyed chestnut tresses of my hair fall around me, shielding me further from his constant scrutiny.

"I'm no one special," I grate out, my rebuttal barely audible. "In fact, I'm more of a hex than an enchantment. Trust me."

"Prefer to trust my own judgment," he disputes. "As humans, we're fundamentally flawed, we choose to see the worst in ourselves. That's not who we are."

I'm fixated on him. The words he speaks, the sound of his voice, the belief in his tone. He's fascinating.

"We favor seeing what we deem as the negative in ourselves. That way we're not surprised when people pull us down, when they judge us. You see a ghost, a *hex*, I see a fucking angel, Zee. Both dark and light fighting for dominance. Your demons are strong, but the light in your soul, it's formidable. I wish you'd stop letting that devil sitting on your shoulder hijack your self-worth."

Pulling the straw from my cup, I push it back down. I repeat the action over and over again, my cheeks burning with the weight in his stare. "You don't know me."

"Not as much as I'd like too, not yet anyway. Still, I'm an observant person. I see what you're trying to hide. I see the pain in your smile, the cautiousness in the way you look at the world."

I remain quiet. Not to be rude. Not by choice. It was all powered by necessity. Truth was I didn't know what to say, or more *how* to say it. Do I thank him for painting me in such a positive light, one I quite frankly didn't deserve? Do I refute his claims? Push him to believe *I* was right.

I see veracity in the words he spoke. People always choose to see the worst in themselves. No matter how often others pushed them to believe otherwise. It's sad really, how much power we offer to our own self-doubt when all we do with our confidence is self-sabotage at every turn.

"Magical powers," he interrupts my thoughts, bringing me back to the moment. "If you could have any, what would it be? Mine?" he continues without offering me the chance to respond. "Would be to read minds. Find out what was swirling in that pretty head of yours."

"I'd want the ability to change the past," I admit quietly.

"Doesn't changing the past completely fuck with the future? Isn't the argument that you *can't* change the future, so eventually, the event you were hell-bent on changing will happen anyway."

I consider his words, a fire of regret burning a hole in my stomach.

"I can't believe that," I argue meekly. "I can't allow myself to believe that my life was always supposed to be this way."

He considers his next words, I see the fight in his eyes, the internal argument he's having with himself, working to determine whether he should vocalize his thoughts. "Taylor," he implores. "Fantasizing about changing the past won't make it happen. I don't claim to know what caused you so much hurt you want to fuck with the universe, but your energy would be better placed with you making your future something you want it to be."

I should feel anger at his words. At the judgment of my life choices. Or more, maybe I *want* to feel anger. Maybe I want to feel judged, to give me a reason to push this man away.

"I'd hate to have the ability to read minds," I change the subject abruptly, no apologies on my lips. "The thought of hearing what everyone thought about me would be horrible."

"Again, you're projecting your self-hate onto others. Who says anyone would think horrible thoughts about you? What about hearing that someone thinks you're beautiful and interesting and that they'd been hoping, *for weeks,* that you'd sit down with them and give them the chance to know you."

"I'd be happy to wait for them to tell me that themselves,

who am I to invade those private thoughts before they're ready to tell me."

He smiles then, the fully-fledged smile, teeth on show, a small bark of laughter echoing the gesture. "If that's the case, I think you're beautiful," he whispers. "And I find you fascinating. I've been coming into this coffee shop with the sole intention of you sitting with me so I could learn more about you. I like you, dove. I like you a lot."

EIGHT

almost five years earlier

"Come on, Zee," Tash pouts, "don't be a party pooper."

I scowl at her back. "I'm not a party pooper, that would suggest I'm not coming out at all."

Dropping her brow pencil, she turns, her half-colored eyebrow rising in challenge. "You're not drinking—"

"I *never* drink," I cut her off on an exaggerated roll of my eyes.

"You're dressed like a nun," she combats.

Glancing down to my jeans and sweater, I frown. "What's wrong with what I'm wearing?"

"Nothing," she scoffs. "If you're fifty and heading out with your mom friends for wine."

I pull at the grey material of my top. It's soft, cuffing at the sleeves, tied at my neck with a silk bow. "It's pretty."

"We're clubbing," she drones. "You want to look *hot,* not pretty."

"I'm confused. Why do I need to look hot? I'm not trying to impress anyone. I want to be comfortable."

Turning back to the mirror, she continues her assault on her eyebrows. "Just because you're getting boned on the regular doesn't mean you can't garner *a little* attention."

"I'm sure Brady would be honored to know he's now affectionately known as my regular *bone* and *not* my boyfriend."

She laughs. "You know what I mean, don't be precious. Just, I don't know, grab something out of my closet, look like you actually *want* to celebrate my birthday."

I groan. "You're insufferable. I need new friends," I complain, moving to her closet.

Climbing from the cab, I readjust Tash's dress.

"Stop." She whacks at my hands. "You look great, stop fidgeting."

The purple material cinches at my waist, flowing out in an airy skirt. The wind tickles my upper thighs and I push the skirt down, groaning internally. My saving grace is that I don't need to keep shifting the dress against my chest, the top is sleeveless, but gathered at my neck, covering my cleavage.

Showing our ID at the door, the security guard waves us through, barely sparing us a glance.

The club is loud, the bass of the music pounding through my ears in a consistent and irritating beat. Bodies are pressed tightly together, and we squeeze past, moving toward the bar in a single line, hands grasped onto the person in front of us.

"Shots?" Tash's sister, Ella, offers, eyes skating over the small number of us.

"Soda and lime," I smile awkwardly.

Ella doesn't give me grief, accepting my reluctance to alcohol without fanfare. Cell out and ready, I aim the camera at their smiling faces, shot glasses poised at their lips. My finger taps the screen, taking snapshot after snapshot of their heads tipping back, the grimace that crosses their faces as their shot burns their throats.

"Jesus, fuck, that shit is nasty," Ella coughs, wiping her mouth with the back of her hand.

"Ladies." A cluster of men approach, drinks in hand, smiles a little lazy, eyes definitely glassy.

Tash turns it on, as is her way, smile flashing, hand to hip as she leans forward to say hello. My friend has *mastered* the art of flirting; the language her body portrays, the purr in her voice, the look in her eye. She's an expert.

I stand comfortably off to the side, letting the group of guys toy their way into buying drinks for my more than eager girlfriends.

"Look at their chests." A voice tickles my ear, and I move away fast, shocked I didn't feel his approach. "All puffed out, working to impress. Like fucking pigeons, preening."

I laugh at his interpretation, considering he's quite right.

Their shoulders are held high, pushed back to accentuate the broadness of their chests.

"I'm Miller." He holds his hand out.

"Zoe." I place my hand in his, shaking it once before letting go.

Face turned to observe our friends, I only catch his profile, but that's all I need to be more than a little enthralled by his beauty. Modelesque. A jawline that the highest paid supermodels in the world would envy, a light dusting of scruff its only imperfection. If you can call it that considering the appeal it adds. *Full* lips, and I mean full; thick cushions pushed out in an exaggerated pout that women nowadays find through injections. He's taller than me by a good six inches, skin tanned and smooth.

I look away, embarrassed by my ogling, not that he seemed to notice, too caught up in watching his friends in amusement.

"Buy you a drink?" He finally looks at me and something in his eyes forces me to shift a step away.

The tiny hairs along the back of my neck stand on end. Call it a sixth sense, I don't know, but the gleam in this guy's eyes is anything but attractive. Chocolate pools of malevolence, a laidback nature, not quite smooth, more *sly* in their attention.

"Uh... no, thank you. I'm good." I lift my still relatively full glass of soda on an awkward smile, turning away.

"Just one," he pushes, moving closer to my body.

Feet shifting closer to Ella, I shake my head. "Honestly, I'm fine. Thank you for offering."

Ella, moving her attention away from her conversation, links her arm in mine. "You okay?"

I nod vigorously. ""Course."

"How's your drink doing?" She waves the guy she was speaking to off, placing her full attention on me.

"Still full," I smile.

"That guy was so painfully boring," she whispers in my ear and I laugh.

"Ugh. His friend was creepy as all hell."

"The hot one?" She glances over my shoulder and I nod.

"He's staring at you."

Chancing a look behind me, my eyes clash with his, and I frown. I wouldn't exactly call what he was doing *staring*. There's a potency to it that's concerning. A *leer,* a fury dancing beneath the surface burning into me. I feel bothered, irritated and disgusted all at once.

"See," I implore, "creepy."

Ella shrugs. "Maybe he's just boozed, or high. People act weird when they're tripping. Ignore him."

An hour later, I feel him at my back. "What's your problem?"

"Huh?" I paint on a smile, forcing myself to look him in the eye.

"I said what's your problem?"

I shake my head, pushing my lips up in an ill-fitting smile. "No problem."

"You rate yourself more than you should. You're not even that hot."

Brows pulling inward, I scowl at him. "Excuse me? I absolutely do *not* think I'm too hot. I'm just not interested. That's not a crime, you know? I have a boyfriend, honestly, you're wasting your time talking to me. I'm sure there's a truckload of more interesting and far better-looking women you could be talking to."

Hand to chest, he feigns shock. "Oh, she's condescending too."

"Everything okay here?" Ella wanders over, hand draped over my shoulder.

"Oh yeah," Miller drawls. "*Zoe* here was just telling me that considering she's not available that I shouldn't worry, that she's sure I could find a nice girl to talk to in this shithole."

Pushing at his chest, Ella steps us backward. "Listen, asshole. I get that you're pretty and that you're not used to women rejecting you, but newsflash, not every woman you come into contact with wants you to fuck her. Chill the fuck out and find some pussy that actually *wants* you."

Turning me away, she grimaces. "Ugh. That guy is a fucking *pig*."

"I might head off," I start, looking at my watch.

"Babe, it's barely ten, and it's Tash's birthday. Don't let one creep ruin your night," she pleads. "Come on, let's dance, get away from the asshole."

I follow her begrudgingly.

An hour later, a sheen of sweat covers my body, and I might be a tiny bit grateful to Tash for forcing me to change out of my jeans and sweater. Standing at the bar, I order another soda and lime, smiling my thanks at the bartender as I pay.

"Hey." A voice sounds at my ear and the smell of the creep's cologne tickles my nostrils. He's standing at my back, pulling away from the bar, I turn.

Hands ripping from the bar with the ferocity of my movements, he holds them up in surrender. "I just wanted to apologize," he placates. "Your friend was right, I'm not exactly used to being rejected..."

Arms crossed over my chest, I nod, accepting his apology wordlessly.

"I'm about to head off, I just didn't feel right leaving without saying sorry. Your boyfriend is a lucky guy," he compliments.

Hands gripping the edge of the bar, he leans closer, forcing my arms to wrap around my body more forcefully. "Enjoy your night, Zoe."

I wait for him to pull back, a tight smile stretching my lips. "Thanks," I grit out, breathing a sigh of relief as he takes a step backward.

He winks and it creeps me the fuck out, enough that I force myself to watch him leave, my nerves crackling over my skin the entire time.

"What a creep," I mumble to myself, turning back to grab my drink, swallowing the contents in three deep gulps.

"That guy bother you again?" Ella pushes against my side a few minutes later, working to get the attention of the bartender.

"No," I worry. "Wanted to apologize."

"Hmm," she pouts. "Did not pick him as the type."

I look back to where I last saw him, leaving the packed nightclub. "Me either."

We stand in relative silence, watching the crowd as Ella sips on her drink. Tash and a few other girls slowly make their way back to where we're standing, focus on the bar and more drinks.

"You okay?" Tash asks and I blink to clear my eyes.

"Nah, I feel like shit," I complain, my vision swaying. "Like I have a migraine coming on."

She speaks again, but her voice sounds foggy, and I shake

my head to try and hear her. The movement turns my stomach and inhaling deeply through my nose, I work to calm the nauseous feeling tickling at my gut. "I'm gonna head off."

Grabbing my purse, I lift my hand, waving goodbye.

"I'll come with you," Ella offers, reaching for her own purse, but I grab her arm, stopping her.

"I'm fine, just tired," I assure her, the slur in my words hidden by the intrusive music echoing through the club.

I force my feet forward, taking measured footsteps as I work to push through the crowd. My head spins slightly and grabbing hold of a random arm to steady myself, I pause.

"Where's the exit?" I ask, eyes focused on my feet, careful not to lose my footing.

The person speaks, but I don't hear what they say, my head fuzzy. Their arm points, letting go of them, I move in the direction they indicated.

A forceful grip holds onto my bicep, and I move to shrug it off. "You're wasted, honey," the deep voice murmurs. "Time to go home."

I glance up, blinking my eyes in an attempt to see him. He's big, a black shirt tight over his chest. He wears an earpiece, it crackles and ducking his shoulder, he speaks. He notions something about escorting someone off premises, and I attempt to move from his grip once again. Unsuccessfully.

"One second, princess, and I'll have you in a cab. Sleep it off."

Fresh air hits my face as we step through the door, and I freeze, righting myself. I inhale deeply through my nose, blinking widely to steady myself. The world around me feels hazy, all I want to do is crawl into bed and sleep for a hundred years.

"Oh, there you are." A voice moves to my side, and the man holding me up, who I can only imagine to be security, pulls me closer.

"You are?"

"Her boyfriend," the voice answers, and I frown because he doesn't sound anything like Brady. "Zoe, baby." A hand fits into mine and I grab hold, using him to keep myself upright.

"Was about to put her in a cab, she's completely out of it," the security guard scolds.

"Mm…" the voice answers. "It was her best friend's birthday, went too hard, too fast, as they do."

Lifting my head, my double-vision encounters two sharp jawlines and I move to pull my hand away, but his grip is too hard. "Miller?" I slur.

"Yeah, baby. It's me," he coos. "Let's get you home. Thanks, buddy," he dismisses my safety net. I try to shake my head, but my body doesn't cooperate.

Miller pulls me forward and I stumble. "No," I argue, my voice catching on the panic in my throat. "St—"

The door of a cab opens and pushing me inside, Miller slides in beside me. I want to scream. I want to cry. I need to move. But everything within me is failing. I can't seem to recall how to speak, my head feeling groggier with every second that passes.

The voice beside me speaks to the driver, but I can't hear a word that's said. Using every last bit of energy I can muster, I lift my head, staring into the rearview mirror, begging the driver to look at me. Silently pleading with me to see the tears in my eyes, to read the panic painted across my face, but he keeps his face averted, eyes focused on the road and *not* me, while I pray for a savior that refuses to see me.

"Shhh," Miller murmurs into my ear, his hand reaching up my skirt. "Don't worry, Zoe, I've got you."

A sob breaks from my lips, but he hollows out the sound with his own, tongue pushing into my mouth against my *feeble* attempt to stop him. Forcing me into the first of many stolen liberties for the evening. A kiss bitterly stolen, a taste of fear so potent in my mouth I feel vomit rushing up my throat, begging for escape. Eyes focused on the rearview mirror, I feel the tight grip of his fingertips cinching my neck.

"Rein it in, bitch," he whispers in my ear so quietly I can barely hear him over the sound of my own choking. "Don't make me hurt you." The wet slide of his tongue traces my earlobe and I wish I could cry. God, I wish my body would fight *with* me.

But the scariest of nightmares is now my life. My body non-responsive, my mind weaving in and out of clarity without design. I'm helpless.

Completely.

Utterly.

Devastatingly.

Helpless.

I beg for my lips to speak, to be *heard*. A pathetic attempt at being *saved* by a stranger that owes me *nothing*.

I'm alone. And that horrific realization is the last thing I remember before it all turns black, his unwelcome mouth on mine, the forceful taste of his tongue burning my lips with an invisible scar I'll carry for eternity.

NINE

"It's been a while since you've wanted to talk about that night," Hannah tests.

I ponder Hannah's statement, considering she's right. More often, I work my hardest to avoid the heart of this very topic.

"I kick myself for not letting Ella come with me that night. I knew something wasn't right. I just *never* imagined I'd been drugged."

"Zoe—" Hannah scolds, but I cut her off.

"I'm not reverting back to my self-blame. Sometimes I just get so mad at myself for how stupid I was in that moment."

"We've been over this," she rebukes. "That's exactly what a low dosage of GHB does, it confuses the victim, muddles their senses."

Eyes focused on the other side of the room, at the blank wall of my loft, I nod. "He knew the right dosage," I mutter. "How frightening is that? He'd perfected the exact dose to mold me into the position he needed." I turn my focus back to the screen. "Do you think he'd done it before?" I push. "Considering how well equipped he was with the exact dosage to keep me relatively *awake* but docile enough to take advantage of."

Hannah pauses for a beat. The seconds dragging with my expectation.

"There's no point dwelling on that."

I roll my eyes. "If he had done it before, how was there no record? Surely another woman has come forward about an attack. And if not, *why?* He could've been stopped before... *before* he—"

"Stop," Hannah cuts me off gently. "Zoe, going over this is no better than the self-blame you were insistent on dressing yourself with just after the attack. It won't bring you any form of peace, you need to focus on moving forward, not looking backward."

"Tripp and I had coffee the other day," I change the subject abruptly, not caring to listen to her lecture me on the importance of looking to the future. "He started his own book club." I chuckle. "Currently it's only he and I in the club, but..." I trail off on a smile, not really sure what else to say.

"Had you told him you like to read?"

I nod. "He was even reading Harry Potter. After our previous conversation, he'd gone away and read the first three books. How crazy is that?"

Her smile is warm. "Not crazy at all. He took something you were interested in and invested his time to get to know you. I'd say he likes you."

"He said that," I mumble. "That he likes me. He told me that."

"Did you tell him that you like him back?"

My head shakes in quick, sharp movements. "No. I didn't

really know *how*. I'm still scared. He challenged me, he challenged my outlook on life and he did so unapologetically. I expected to be mad at the push he seemed so hell-bent on giving me, but I wasn't. Why?"

"You've never come across irritated at me when *I* push you?"

I sigh. "That's because I feel comfortable with you. I know your words aren't laced in judgment."

Tucking her hair behind her ear, I watch her eyebrows reach her hairline and I laugh softly.

"You think I feel the same way when I'm with Tripp."

She shrugs. "You're the one who said it. I'm just asking you to *see* it."

"Did I tell you about the book I read recently?"

Leaning back in her seat, Hannah shakes her head. "No."

"It's been made into a Netflix series. About a guy who stalks a girl he meets in a bookstore." My gaze skates over my couch, in search of the book to show her.

"I've seen the series," she breaks off my search, and I look back at my computer screen. "You read the book?" The shock in her voice is clear.

"Yeah," I confirm confidently. "There were moments that I had to put it down, but I got through it without having a panic attack. Maybe that's not a big deal," I shrug, suddenly feeling uncertain of my point, of the power I thought I'd claimed back in a way.

"There's a predator in the story. One disguised in plain sight. I'd say it's a *huge* deal that it didn't trigger you. My question is why you chose to read that book in the first place? Were you testing yourself?"

"Book club," I answer. "It was Rae's suggestion and I

didn't want to stir up any questions as to why I wouldn't be comfortable with her choice... so I sucked it up."

"You could've just skipped the next catch up," she offers.

My shoulders lift, only to drop back down heavily. "I didn't want to. I like being around them, I didn't want to fail before I'd even *tried.*"

It's moments like these I curse our sessions are completed via Skype, not being able to read her as well as if I were in the room. I can't *feel* her energy. I just have to *guess* based on her facial cues. Considering she's one of the most passive people I've ever known, saying that feat is impossible is an understatement.

"Zoe Lincoln, welcome back to your life." The sentence is delivered with pride I've never heard Hannah use before, and it makes me laugh.

"You can laugh all you want," she echoes the sound. "It's the truth. Look at you, stepping out of your comfort zone to establish friendships, working to nurture them as best you can. Not only that, you're willingly conversing with a man who seems to have a romantic interest in you, which you, by all appearances, share. You're smiling more than I've ever seen. You're *happy,* Zoe."

Her words filter into my psyche and I consider she's right. I am happy, or in this moment I *feel* happy.

"You've finally remembered that you're *alive.*"

A smile breaks at my lips and I cover my face to hide my embarrassment.

"Don't hide," she implores. "I'm so proud of you."

"Thank you," I whisper, dropping my hands into my lap. "Where do I go from here?" My smile drops away, genuine concern leaking into my veins. "With Tripp," I clarify. "We can't spend the rest of our lives in Caffeine Coma but venturing out of that bubble is unnerving."

"I wouldn't suggest putting yourself in a position where you feel *alone* with him so early on in your relationship. Being at a restaurant, in a park, in a movie theater... you're surrounded by people."

"I was surrounded by people in the bar," I whisper shakily.

"Different circumstance, Zoe. Think about places you'd deem as *safe*. *When* he asks you out, you choose the venue. Set the pace, with everything."

"Will I push him away by being so, I don't know, flaky?"

Her head tips to the side. "I'm putting on my friend hat here in place of my therapist one... If he's perturbed by you setting the pace, he's not worth it."

Nodding, I offer her a complacent smile. "You're right. I really like him. I don't want to screw it up because I'm screwed up."

"We're all a little broken, Zoe. Tripp will have his flaws. Trust me."

"I read up on fantasy baseball."

Tripp's face lights up at my voice, his face turning to bring me into view.

He really is handsome. Classically so. A man that turns heads, that causes women to double-take, knowing they didn't have enough time to appreciate his beauty in that fleeting glance. No matter how often I see him, which is almost daily, his effect doesn't lessen. He renders me speechless, and based on the smirk traveling all the way to his eyes, he knows it. More, he likes it.

"And?" he prompts.

Sitting beside him, not across from him as has been my norm for weeks now, my lips twist in thought. "I have questions," I confess. "At the beginning of your season, you select players for your league, correct?"

"Correct," he confirms.

"What if you and another member of your league want the same player? How do you decide on who gets them?"

Leaning forward, his hand taps my knee. "We auction at the beginning of the season," he explains.

"You outbid if you really want someone," I clarify, and he nods.

"Exactly."

"You play rotisserie?"

Squeezing my knee softly, he laughs. "You have done your research. I'm impressed."

I shrug. "You read three Harry Potter books, least I could do."

He likes that. Appreciates that I noticed the effort he placed in knowing me better, more now that I've done the same.

"Yes, my league plays rotisserie," he answers. "It's online, unfortunately, the guys I play with are from all over. Would be nice to argue it out in person though."

"You bet money on your season?"

"Mm-hmm," he hums. "A little wager we each throw in."

It's only then that I notice his hand hasn't moved from my knee, the warmth of his palm felt through my jeans. My first reaction is to move, to force his hand to drop away. I stop myself though, my mind working to decide if I hate it. Shockingly, I don't. Not in the slightest. In fact, I enjoy the feel of him touching me and the small show of affection offered in his simple touch. My gaze drops to his hand, pulling his attention to the place in which our bodies connect.

"Have dinner with me?"

Looking up at him through my lashes, I exhale my nerves, inhaling the confidence he seems to bring out in me with a simple look.

"I'd like that."

"Tomorrow night?" he murmurs.

I agree silently with a quick nod of my head.

"Can I pick you up, or..."

"I'll meet you there," I combat.

"Perfect," he hums. "I'll just need a phone number, email, something to be able to contact you, to send you the details."

Pulling his cell from his pocket, he unlocks the screen, handing it to me.

Staring at the phone in my hand, butterflies in my stomach, my thumb works across the screen. He laughs when I hand it back, my number saved under the nickname he's bestowed upon me.

"Ever told you I like you, dove?"

"No," I tease, shocked at the ease in which the jibe comes from my mouth. "I don't think you have."

"Well, I do." He stands only to crouch beside me, taking my hand in his. "A lot," he whispers. Eyes anchored, he pushes himself up, leaning over me. Frozen in place, the anticipation of his touch is as exhilarating as it is frightening. My breath is caught in my lungs, needing release, but I'm unable to find it.

The soft push of his lips kisses against my cheek, holding there for a second before pulling away. A breath of space hangs between us, the not-quite-blue pools of his eyes fixed on mine. "We take this as slow as you need it to go."

A wave of emotion hits me like a tsunami, drowning me in the unfamiliar feelings coursing through my veins.

This man is *everything* women dream about. Everything *I* dream about. He's kind and patient. A soul seemingly as pretty as his face.

I don't know how I caught Tripp Tanner's eye. I don't know how he came to find himself in the coffee shop I work in. I certainly don't know why my body responds to him in a way I never thought it would with a man again. All those questions and uncertainty aside, all I can muster is that I'm thankful all the same. Grateful for the kind soul that is as magnetized to mine as I am his.

TEN

Laying on my bed, Rae shakes her head at the dress I pull from my closet. "Nah."

"You bullied your way over with the pretense of helping me get ready for my date, and you've said no to everything. You're being *far* from helpful, more a hindrance."

She laughs, her joy giving way to a sneer as my cat brushes against my leg and jumps onto my bed.

"You know cats are evil, yeah?"

Dress shoved back into my closet, I roll my eyes. "That so?"

"Absolutely. The world knows it, too. Think of every animated film in existence, I ain't ever seen a hero cat. They're always the villain."

It's my turn to laugh. "We taking life lessons from animated films now?"

"Uh, yeah," she bristles, standing as Potter moves closer to her. "Disney is my fucking bible, bish."

I chuckle, the sound getting away from me and turning into a full body laugh.

"What are you laughing at?" She ruffles.

"Badass Rae is afraid of a wittle-kitty-cat," I babble to Potter, picking him up and kissing his fur.

"I'm not afraid," she quips. "Carefully cautious. That cat was aiming to scratch my fucking eyeballs out."

Placing the cat back on my bed, I shake my head. "Hardly. He's too lazy to consider such strenuous activity. What was wrong with that dress?"

Dropping into the oversized armchair in the corner of the room, she throws her legs over one arm, arching her back over the other. She looks at me upside down. "You cringe every time you pick up a dress. Why are you trying to be someone you're not comfortable with?"

"It's a date... I... God, I don't know, maybe I should just cancel."

Bolting upright, she throws a pillow at me. "What's wrong with just wearing what you're comfortable in?" She laughs. "He digs you when you're wearing jeans and a t-shirt at the coffee shop. He doesn't care what you wear."

I sigh. "How do you know that?"

"Do you give a shit what he turns up in tonight?"

My eyebrows pull together. "Of course not."

Hands flipping over to show her palms, she looks at me expectantly. "Then trust me when I tell you he doesn't care either. He just wants to spend time with you."

Rae leaves the room, leaving me to dress and yanking on a pair of jeans and a white blouse and follow after her.

"This okay?"

Head bent over my drawings, she glances up. "Why the fuck do you work in the coffee shop?" She wanders over, eyes scaling my body. Grabbing the waist of my jeans, she tucks the blouse in the band, moving around me to tuck it in the whole way around. Stepping back from my body, lip tipped out in consideration, she nods. "Cool with that?"

Turning toward the mirror at the front door, I twist one way and then the other. Hmm. "Yeah." I sound surprised. "Question."

"Answer," she jibes, and I roll my eyes.

"What's up with you and Tamra?"

She groans.

"What? You're constantly niggling at her, but I see you watch her. You're into her."

"Observant," she muses. "We hooked up once, she freaked about being with a woman. Her strategy is now to avoid me at all costs."

"She does a terrible job," I offer, feeling really bad for Rae.

"I try not to read into it. I like her. A lot. I don't know why, she's moody as fuck. But she's so fucking beautiful and the way she talks; about books, life, music... she's passionate. I just wish she wasn't ashamed of being attracted to the same sex."

"Is she?" I push. "Ashamed? Or just confused?"

She shrugs. "Does it matter? She won't give me the time of day. I nag at her to get her to crack, well that's my current game plan. I tried being nice, tried being indifferent. She stares at me, sometimes she'll text me, reels me in only to spit me out before actually hooking me."

I frown. "That's not very nice."

"Want me to curl your hair?" She changes the subject and respecting her wishes, I let her, stopping the conversation, feeling a little less warm toward Tamra than I did two minutes ago.

Touching the hair falling around my shoulders, I shrug and nod at the same time. "Sure."

Standing in front of Rae in my bathroom, she waits for the hair straightener to heat up.

"I work in the coffee shop to force myself to be around people. I'm a homebody. A hermit. Socializing isn't really my thing, I'm too awkward. But, life gets lonely," I admit sadly. "It's just a change of scenery a few days a week," I answer her question from earlier.

Sectioning my hair, she piles a heap atop of my head, securing it with a clip. I watch her hands move, the twist in her wrist as she curls my hair around the hot iron, pulling it through to let a loose curl unfurl along my shoulder.

Winking at my reflection, she focuses back on my hair. "You a natural brunette?"

I shake my head, causing her to frown. "Sorry." I stop moving. "Blonde."

"Next time you dye it, call me, please. You've missed a patch at the back here."

"Oh my God, really?" My hand moves to grab at my hair, and she smacks it away.

"It's underneath, you can't see."

Wrist twisted against my hair, my eyes are too focused on her hands to notice her body lock solid. Pulling the iron from my head, she shifts my hair out of the way, a finger running along the semicolon tattooed behind my ear.

Our eyes clash against our reflections and I'm thankful for the mirror. The cut of glass between us and reality where I can let her see my demons without feeling the harsh existence of pity on her breath.

She looks away first, unpinning the pile of hair she had

trapped at the top of my head. I watch her section the strands once again, lost in thought as she artfully maneuvers the iron through my hair.

"How long ago?" She finally speaks, the sound of her voice a dull echo in the confines of the bathroom walls.

"A few years," I answer without thinking. "I didn't attempt..." I trail off, rolling my shoulders. "I thought about it though."

She watches me in our reflection.

"There was a man... he..."

She's the first person, Hannah aside of course, I've ever openly spoken to about what happened. Since the trial ended some four years ago anyway. Maybe it's because we're locked away in a bubble, cramped within the walls of my bathroom, that pushes me into a sense of security. Maybe it's because it's her, and she's the first person that's cared enough to pursue a friendship since I walked away from my life.

"Did you get justice?" She understands what I can't bring myself to vocalize.

Looking down at my bare feet, she doesn't scold me for moving, just shifts herself to allow her to continue with my hair.

"Some would say so," I confess. "But I disagree."

My hair finished, she slides the straightener along my bathroom counter, fingers grasping the side of my head to lift it delicately. "How long did he serve?"

I let the single tear fighting for escape fall down my cheek. "Three years."

Her big eyes darken in hate, nostrils flaring in irritation, but she doesn't speak. She doesn't need to.

"Did you know him?" The question is whispered so quietly, I can barely hear her.

I don't speak. I can't. Words like acid flowing through my vocal cords, making it painful enough to not even try. Instead, I shake my head, a quick back and forth that answers for me.

There's no declaration of injustice or apology for what happened to me. There's no judgment or pity in her eyes. She's mad for me, but she doesn't vocalize that and I'm grateful. I'm her friend, and in that simple raw and open moment, she proves that by allowing me to be the girl she met at a book club. Not a victim. Not someone to pity.

"Boots?" I change the subject, my eyes begging her to let me.

The thing about Rae Saito that I've come to learn is that she reads silent cues better than others. More, she respects the hell outta them.

Taking my abrupt change of subject with ease, she steps back. "Absolutely. You'll need a jacket too, it's cool out."

She follows my exit from the bathroom, moving back to my desk.

"Never would've picked you as an artist," she ponders as I come out of my room, boots, and jacket in hand. "But now that I *see* you, it just, I don't know, fits?"

I smile in place of answering, dropping to my couch to pull my boots on.

"What time were you meeting Tripp?"

"Eight," I answer, standing to shimmy into my jacket.

"You look great, T."

I stop, hands falling to my side as I consider my new friend. More the fact that after too long, I actually have someone I trust enough to let into my life. My relationship with Rae hasn't been forced, it just... *was, is* rather. From our initial meeting a few months back she's become a beacon of hope. Someone who always seems to be there. She texts me funny memes if she thinks I'll like them. She sends me horrible cat memes, working to prove my cat is plotting my demise. She asks me out for breakfast. She drops by unannounced to watch movies, and shockingly, I'm *okay* with it. More than okay, I miss her when she's not around.

In a moment that I'd normally shut down completely, I felt composed enough to open up, even slightly. Rae had earned my trust, my respect, by being comfortable in what I was willing to share. She didn't pry. She didn't push. She asked, I answered. End of story.

Clearing my throat, I grab her attention, and she pulls her focus from my drawings. "I have something to tell you, but I need to know that it will only *ever* be between you and me. It's something no one around here knows, and I aim to keep it that way."

"Oookay," she murmurs, turning to give me her full attention.

"Only reason I'm telling you this is that I think we're friends, actually, you're probably the best I've got, the best I've had in a really long time."

Worry lines her face and if I wasn't so overwhelmed by what I was about to share, I'd laugh at how much I'm freaking her out.

"My name isn't Taylor," I confess, and I watch as her worry lines smooth, giving way to her eyebrows as they reach her hairline. "I changed it, after everything that happened. I wanted a fresh start, I wanted who I was to be forgotten."

"Why are you telling me then?" she queries quietly, leaning against my desk.

"Because I don't want our friendship to begin on a lie," I test. "It was easy to go by another name when people I cared about weren't calling me it on the regular. But having someone I classify as a friend call me a name that isn't *mine*..." I trail off on a shrug.

"Makes sense... so...."

"Zoe," I introduce myself. "Zoe Lincoln."

Her full lips stretch into a wide grin. "Nice to meet you, Zoe Lincoln. And if we're sharing secrets that are to be kept in this room" —she holds out her pinky, which I wrap mine around— "my full name is Raelene, and if you *ever* tell a soul that, I'll harvest your organs."

I laugh when I should feel bare. Raw at the use of my real name. But I don't. I feel almost empowered. Silly, considering the fact that I know Rae will never use my real name except for in the confines of these walls when it's just her and I. But the girl I was so sure I'd buried years ago is bubbling under the surface of this persona I've been hell-bent on building over the years, and fuck me if it doesn't feel good to claim a little bit of myself back.

ELEVEN

First dates. The holy grail of disastrous opportunity. A sliver in time where you aim to put the *very* best version of yourself on show. The single most exhausting and mundane of human interaction. The get-to-know-you. *Cringe.*

A small window of time spent, where at the end you have to decide... *do* you take the gamble? *Is* this person *worth* the risk?

Everyone has watched a first date unfold in apt amusement. We pinpoint them in restaurants, giggling amongst ourselves. Taking bets on whether they'll go the distance or whether one or both are texting a friend on the sly, *begging* them to save them with a falsified emergency that lets them escape without inflicting those dreaded hurt feelings. Shit, maybe you've been their voice-over, playing with your more established significant other as if your relationship is of higher standing. A night's entertainment, the only cost the expense of the poor souls taking a chance on a happily ever after.

I started the night in a relatively positive frame of mind,

but since Rae left my apartment, my mood is changing. A dark cloud of despondency has set in above me, refusing to move.

I've tried to shake it. But I'm on my way to that very same social experiment, expecting to fail and I can't pinpoint my why. In truth, this first date should be easy in comparison to the experiences of others. Tripp and I aren't strangers per se. Sure, we don't *know* one another. But we have a foundation, a budding friendship of sorts.

It's the expectation I think. The *pressure*. This *ridiculous* need to impress. When really, if everyone were just themselves from the get-go, we could make an educated decision whether to move forward. Save us the tumultuous in-between. The failure. The disappointment.

Ugh.

I forced an impromptu session with Hannah earlier today. Like always and not surprisingly, she drilled it into me to be myself.

Sounds simple, right?

Pft. This is the hardest thing for us humans to do. Be our perfectly flawed selves. But how can we expect someone else to love us when more often than not we despise ourselves? Maybe not completely, but enough to seek validation and approval from others. Slap a label of love over the top and people froth at the *need* to feel it.

Personally, I think I share the opinion that until you love yourself. Until you're content and happy with the person you are... You can't expect someone else to love you.

But I've tried that, loving myself. It's been a sour realization of mine to learn that I can't seem to do it on my own. I need a reminder, as selfish as that sounds. I need to see what he does. What is it about me that captures his attention enough to keep coming back? I need someone to teach me how to love myself. It's depressing as all hell, but I need someone else to remind me of why I'm worthy.

I had a boyfriend before Miller. What a definition to hold; Zoe Lincoln's Origin of Life - before Miller and after Miller.

Anyway, I had a boyfriend. Brady. He was a typical college jock. But he was charming, and he wormed his way into my life with hideous jokes and cheesy one-liners. He once told me that I took his breath away the first time he saw me. It made me blush. He liked doing that, making me blush. He nicknamed me *thief.* Brady was a *good* guy and the time I spent with him, I felt invincible.

Brady built my self-worth *so* fucking high I never imagined how diabolical the fall from that height of self-love could be. Worse, how hard the climb back up would be.

We often spoke of the life we'd have. What our wedding would look like, how many kids we'd have, where we'd live. God, we were so naïve. We'd experienced no roadblocks in our relationship, shit, there'd barely been speedbumps in the two years we spent loving one another.

Until Miller.

After Miller.

It all changed then. The sunshine that seemed to follow us around had darkened in a way neither of us could ignore in the end. Thick and angry clouds swirling around us in a tornado of uncertainty and pain. We were being dragged by our teeth, holding on out of obligation. The burden of the bond we once shared hovering above us in hope. We were there once, surely our love was strong enough to take us there again.

There was a time where I was confident, content, happy

in my life. Brady was a *big* part of that. I imagine that he thought he'd loved me hard enough once, that continuing on that same path would be enough to help me heal.

It just wasn't enough. I'd fallen so far off the ledge of happiness and he was *there* reaching out, trying to pull me back, but I wouldn't reach back. I *couldn't* reach back. I was too weak. The demons of my mind hijacking every thought convincing me I no longer deserved him or the love he so eagerly wanted to offer me.

Love.

Without doubt or question, the *most* complicated of all human emotions.

People vow it's the greatest feeling in the world. What they don't tell you is that it's also the most painful. Not to forget likely the most dangerous as well. A mental state so powerful, it leaves you at your weakest. Unguarded. Bared. The sharpest of double-edged swords. A feeling so intense, so strong it offers you completion. You have *everything*.

Until you don't.

That's the kicker. Nothing lasts forever. The question is whether you're willing to gamble your own self-worth on something that holds an indeterminable expiry date. Because while love may offer you fulfillment, it also has the capacity to strip you raw. It has the capability to *destroy* you.

Miller may have stabbed me with the first and most poignant knife of hate, but Brady kept inflicting wound after wound by staying, by trying to love me back to myself. It hurt too much; watching him fail, my rejection, my pure and utter resistance in *wanting* to be better.

Love will pull you in with its promise of ever-after. That glimmer of happiness so bright you can't imagine feeling anything else. It's the ultimate joke on human nature. Blinding us of our own flaws, by our own stupid insecurity of being alone.

Do you love me?

I couldn't tell you how many times Brady asked me that in the lead up to our demise.

Do you love me?

We've heard it before, and we balk when the recipient of such a question can't answer. Of course, we would, because how could you *not* want to fall in love. The thought around it seems simple enough. Either you do or you don't.

Please.

It's not simple. Not at all. You're asking someone whether they're willing to put their own happiness aside for yours. A fight for dominance. Who reigns supreme in your world is what you're really asking... you or me.

Love is without condition. That's another good one.

Brady and I were in love. Once upon a time. Or maybe by definition, we weren't. Maybe we only cared for one another to a limit. In the end, our *love* wasn't without condition.

I had my conditions. He could love me, but he couldn't touch me.

He had his conditions. He couldn't love me *without* touching me.

Where did that leave us?

I wasn't invincible, not like my imaginary bubble of love made me believe. Being with Brady wasn't powerful enough to stop some asshole in a bar from raping me.

Maybe neither Brady or I loved one another. I couldn't put his happiness above my suffering. It wasn't as important. It was the only thing I knew how to do at that time in my life. I wanted to be there because the alternative of climbing that mountain to find the Zoe that I once was, was too big of a task for me to conquer. Before you label me the jerk in this scenario, he was the same. He couldn't accept the newly defined conditions of our relationship, he tried, it just didn't make *him* happy.

Or maybe, just maybe, we loved one another enough to let go. Maybe my over cynical heart has let me blacken the deep crimson river of passion. Hannah's right, in the years following my attack, I've let it define me. There's definitely no rose colored glasses in my arsenal. There's only black and white, fuck even the gray area.

"We're here."

The Uber driver pulls me from my depressing thoughts, and I nod my thanks, climbing from his car. Standing on the sidewalk, I stare at the restaurant I'm meeting Tripp at, considering reopening the Uber app to find a car to take me straight back home.

The shrill ringtone of my phone shocks me and reaching into my purse, I pull it out.

"You're freaking out, aren't you?"

I half laugh, half sigh at Rae's teasing. "Yes."

"Stop overthinking it. You enjoy this guy's company over coffee, what's the difference in enjoying it over dinner?"

I turn my back on the restaurant. "It seems more formal."

"Zoe," she breathes. "If you're looking for a reason to stop this from eventuating, you're gonna find one. But you like this guy, he intrigues you, he challenges you, he's hot," she adds.

"I'm scared."

"Of what?"

I clear my throat. "That he'll think I'm too much work."

"Fuck him if he thinks that," she grumbles. "People come with baggage, bet your evil cat Tripp's got plenty of his own. Don't convince yourself he thinks a certain way before you've given him the chance to make his own decision, it's not fair on him."

She takes in my silence. "Have fun, Zoe. Share a meal with an interesting guy and if it's horrible and painful, don't do it again. Stop living in that warzone of your mind and just fucking *live* or I'll tell Dex you want a makeover."

"Oh God," I laugh. "Please don't."

TWELVE

Tripp is caught in conversation with a waiter as I enter the restaurant, giving me ample opportunity to watch him candidly. The animated way in which he speaks, completely invested in the man holding his attention. I like that about him. He rarely lets himself be distracted by the world around him. He allows himself to be captivated by the moment.

Laughing at something the waiter says, he throws his head back, his scratchy chuckle echoing through the room more pleasant than any melody. It catches the attention of the people around him, not that he notices, too caught up in his amusement to give anyone a second thought. He's confident in himself, in who he is. Another thing I admire.

I watch the way women appreciate him, not that I blame them. He's beautiful, and not just to look at. The way he holds himself is an ode to kindness. He smiles at strangers, holds doors open, pulls faces at little kids to make them laugh. He'd give up his seat on the subway no hesitation, help old ladies cross the street, I'm certain of it. There's inherent *goodness* in his soul and it shines pretty heavily in his eyes. Add that to the pretty package all that virtuousness is wrapped up in and it's no surprise women are attracted to him.

Hand extended, the waiter grasps it, shaking it. Tripp watches him walk away before checking his watch. It's then I notice his nerves, the uncertainty making him fidget. Chancing a glance at the door he catches sight of me, and his nerves dissipate almost immediately.

He was afraid I wouldn't show.

He smiles. The big one, teeth on show, laugh lines heavily indented in his handsome face.

He reaches me in three quick strides. "Zee, you came."

"Sorry I'm late," I offer in greeting.

Hands lifting in a gesture of dismissal, he lets a hand reach up to cup my cheek, watching me for a split second of time. "You look beautiful." The soft brush of his lips against my cheek causes my eyes to close.

I haven't kissed a man in years, not since Brady and I ended. Even then, after the attack, it was only once, and it ended disastrously. Both of us rushing into a poorly executed plan to erase the damage and pain we'd both been pushed into.

But this, the tender and sparing touches of Tripp's lips on my skin fires something inside of me I thought had died. My *lust*. My *want*. My *need*.

Eyes fluttering open, I let my gaze fall on his face. Not one to let his feelings hide, the thoughts swirling heavily in my mind are like an open book on Tripp.

"Smell good, dove," he murmurs, dragging his fingers over a lock of my hair.

Hand placed in the bow of my lower back, Tripp makes a move forward, but I step from his touch.

The cab. The push for me to bend to his will. The burning touch of his palm against my back propelling me into the back seat, to where my nightmare only just began.

"I don't like that. Being guided," I admit shamefully. "It may seem odd..." I close my eyes to shut out the look I'm certain is on his face. "But..."

"You *never* have to apologize for something that makes you uncomfortable. I respect you, which means I respect your boundaries."

Eyes flashing open, he chuckles at the shock in my reaction. He steps forward, gesturing toward our table, but I remain stationary, staring at him in awe.

I have no clue as to why he is the way he is. *Why* he's so considerate, so respectful of my needs. I could read into it, convince myself there was more to the story than meets the eye. Tell myself he has an ulterior motive, but I don't believe that. Not for a second. My belief rests solely in the fact that Tripp is just an inherently kind human being.

"Dove?" He glances back, confusion marring is otherwise perfect face.

"I like you a lot, too." There's a vehemence in my words, a vow in the way I speak. One I hope he reads well enough to believe I'm worth the trouble.

The confusion that had pulled his brows heavily together eases, replaced by a smile that makes my heart flutter in my chest.

"Was hoping so. Come, let's eat."

Settled at the table, the waiter Tripp was talking to moments ago approaches.

"Tripp, you lie, she's even more beautiful than you said."

I duck my head in embarrassment, only to lift it again, smiling my thanks at his compliment.

For years I've tried to hide in the shadows, to be invisible to the world. The beauty that others saw in me, I saw as a curse. A glamor to hide the ugly and disgusting truth about who I really was.

"Didn't want you to try and steal her away, Nico."

As the years have passed me by, my self-disgust has faded. There are times I still feel tainted, *dirty*. Flashes in time where I shower *far* too often, the act morphing into an obsession. One that forces me to scrub at my skin until it's red and raw, to remove the memory of his touch.

But for Tripp, I don't want to be that person I at times let myself become. He makes me *want* to be the beauty he sees. Gone is the broken down girl, pieces of her once whole-self scattered along the floor in disregard. Instead, my shattered pieces are slowly lifting from the ground they've been resting comfortably on. Coming together piece by broken piece to build a *new* whole. Someone a little different, sure, the scars of where I've been glued back together invisible to the naked eye, but obvious if you look hard enough at the person I now am.

"Way she looks at you, friend," Nico pulls me from my thoughts, "*impossible*." The man would be nearing sixty; silver hair adorning his head, his stomach rotund, pushed heavily against the pressed black slacks he's wearing.

"Taylor," Tripp starts. "This is Nico, an old family friend. Nico, this is my dove." While his words are directed toward his friend, his focus is set solely on me, a soft and intimate warmth to his features pulling me in.

My dove.

"Nice to meet you, sweet girl. Now." He ignores the fact that Tripp and I are completely caught up in ourselves. "I insist you settle on a *Merlot*, I have one," he moans. "Vinified locally, exquisite."

Reluctantly, I pull from Tripp's snare, looking to Nico. "While it sounds lovely, I think I might just stick with water if that's okay."

"Same for me, Nico."

"No." I grab Tripp's hand. "Please. Don't miss out on my account, you'll break Nico's heart."

He watches me for a beat. "I can try it any time. Sparkling, okay?"

He must see me grimace before I can school it, a bark of laughter breaking from his lips. "Tap it is. Thanks, bud."

The waiter offers a slight dip of his head before disappearing.

"Really, Tripp." I squeeze his hand, trying hard not to consider that I haven't let it go. "You could've had wine. Just because I don't drink doesn't mean you have to miss out."

Leaning in, his tongue darts out to wet his lips. "I know I could've had it, I'm happy with water. I like your hair out like that," he murmurs, changing the subject while his gaze skates along the barrel curls surrounding my face.

"A little different from the ponytail," I grin.

"I like the ponytail, too."

"You compliment a lot."

That earns me a chuckle. "I say what I feel, what I think. Someone once told me rather than having the ability to read thoughts, they'd prefer to wait until that person was ready to tell them what was in their mind."

My cheeks shade.

"This is me letting you into my thoughts."

"I like your laugh," I offer my own compliment. "When I walked in tonight, I was brimming with anxiety. I can't remember the last time I was this nervous... Then I heard you laugh, and it settled the tempest within me."

Tongue darting out to wet his lips, his eyes shutter closed on a shy grin. "Like the insight into your thoughts, dove."

Nico approaches our table, water in hand. We settle into a comfortable silence as he fills our glasses. Placing the bottle on the table, Tripp asks him to give us a little more time and he walks away without saying a word, a small bow to his head.

"Tell me about the UK."

Shifting his cutlery to the side, he leans closer, jaw rested lightly on his hand.

"I think I told you my mom is a bit of a nomad," he smiles affectionately, a lot of love caught in the gesture. "She traveled a lot when I was a kid, I went with her often. My time was split between her and my dad. She lived in the UK for a stint and I fell in love.

"I worked in the heart of London, which was dreary and busy but also bustling and diverse and *home.*" His left shoulder lifts. "It was the smaller townships that really captured my heart. The quaint country sides. The color of the grass and the freshness in the air." He hums, inhaling heavily as if he can smell it now, the scent of fresh rain and cut grass. "It's something else, Zee."

"Why come back?" I question, folding my napkin into a square.

"My dad wants me to take over his business eventually. I needed to be present, to begin the transition from absent son to managing partner." His eyes fall to the folded napkin.

Lifting it, I lay it across my lap, removing it from temptation. "What about you? Have you traveled much?"

I shake my head. "Not really. I grew up in Charlottesville, attended college close by. I'd been to Manhattan before with my family, so when it came time to move away, I wanted somewhere I semi-knew. Somewhere I wouldn't feel so lost."

"You don't feel lost in New York City?"

Disbelief. Shock. They're not unrealistic reactions.

Lifting my water, I take a sip, watching him over the rim of my glass. He waits patiently, eyes never venturing anywhere but my face.

Setting my glass back down, I drag a finger down the condensation. "I like being invisible. Manhattan lets me reach that level of anonymity. Yes, I feel like I'm easily lost, but that's what I want, which," I laugh, "sounds so silly, but it makes me feel settled."

"Another face in the crowd," he guesses.

"Yeah." I push my glass away. "Just a face without a name. Needle in a haystack."

"Are you hiding?"

"Mostly from myself," I admit without thinking. "What's your favorite place in the world?" I change the subject before he can dig further into my psyche, afraid I'll give him more than I'm ready to.

"Easy." He takes my direction without issue. "Australia."

"You've been to Australia?" I balk. "What is that, like a fifteen-hour flight?"

"Give or take an hour, yeah."

"Wow. Are there kangaroos jumping around the streets?"

He laughs, the rich sound dancing between us like a magnet, pulling me closer.

"No. It's a falsehood, a damn shame too."

"I've heard pretty much everything you come across can kill you."

The laugh again, this time loud enough to pull the attention of the surrounding tables. Not that he noticed, he's too focused on me.

"I came out unscathed." His amusement dies down. "It's so beautiful, dove. Coastal towns with the prettiest beaches you've ever seen."

"I've never seen the beach," I confess.

"You haven't?" He stops short, a groan forcing his dark eyebrows to his hairline. "Baby, I need to take you. The soft grains of sand between your toes, sun kissing your skin." His eyes close. "It has this sound, like a song no one could *ever* recreate. The crash of waves against the shore, the call of the seagulls, shit, the *wide* open space, it's the greatest fucking melody."

Opening his eyes, he sighs in longing. "The way your skin feels after swimming in the ocean is like nothing else. The salt sticks to your skin, it feels tight and you feel dry and wet all at the same time."

"You paint a very enticing picture, I'm now craving an ocean I've never seen."

"But if I take you to Australia first," he combats, "you'll be ruined for all other beaches. Not that it's a bad thing. There's no substitute for perfection, dove."

The way he finishes his sentence makes me believe he's no longer talking about the beach, the color of his irises warming into a blue not dissimilar to the sea he longs for.

"You don't give a thought to second-place when you're

staring down first." His hand touches mine, his calloused thumb running over my knuckles affectionately.

First place. Sitting here with me, in a crowded restaurant, hand clasped around mine Tripp Tanner sees me as the grand prize and I'd be lying if I said I wasn't, in that moment, feeling the exact same way.

Walking through my front door, I lock it. All three separate locks. Forcing myself to do it methodically. Slowly. Ensuring I know, without doubt, that my space is secured from intruders; both real and the ones that reside in my head.

Potter brushes through my legs, purring softly.

"Hey, buddy." I pick him up, kissing his fur. "Miss me?"

He struggles out of my hold, breaking my fragile heart. "Have I ever told you that you really suck as a companion?"

My conceited cat walks about without sparing me a second glance, tail raised in the air like the haughty prince he is.

Cell sounding in my bag, I retrieve it, my cat's dismissal easily forgotten at Tripp's name lighting up my screen.

Tripp: I hope this doesn't come across too

forward, but having to say goodbye tonight was like torture. I'd say it was a fantastic first date, but I'm claiming our coffee dates as our firsts. xx

Dove: I can't remember the last time I enjoyed myself as much. Thank you. Really. I had a wonderful time. x

Tripp: I'll be having breakfast at the Waldorf tomorrow around 9am before a meeting. I wouldn't have any objections at someone with pretty green eyes joining me... if you're free?

I stare at his message, my eyes all but bugging out of my head.

Tripp: That was too much, wasn't it? I'm sorry for coming on too strong.

Dove: Not at all. I'd love that. I'll see you at 9.

Tripp: I look forward to it, dove. Sleep well.

THIRTEEN

"So you went on a date, and not an hour after you got home he texted you to ask you out again? For the next morning?"

I nod at Dex's question.

"Holy fucking shit, you're a magician. Teach me," he begs, making me laugh.

"Please tell me he's a maniac in the sack as well as a hopeless romantic?"

Looking around to make sure no one heard, I frown over at my friend. Rae hits him over the head. "Jesus, Dex, have some fucking tact."

"Sorry." He ducks his head, looking ashamed. "Sometimes I just..." His hand moves away from his mouth in an indication of verbal vomit.

"It's okay, honestly... we haven't even kissed."

"*Fucking magician,*" he mutters, shaking his head in awe. "Lemme get this straight, you threw coffee at the guy the first time you met?"

I nod.

"Then after your first conversation you —in a roundabout

way— attacked his choice of profession and then didn't speak to him for a month?"

"Mmhmm," I agree.

"Since then you've been having coffee two or three times a week, you've been on one *official* date and you haven't touched. *At all*."

"We've held hands," I admit defensively. "And he's kissed my cheek."

Dex blinks at me like an owl, his too big eyes wide in disbelief. "Is this guy even real?"

Rae laughs then. "I saw him once. He's hot as fuck, too."

"Of course he is," Dex sighs. "Excuse me while I head over to Caffeine Coma and wait for my fucking Prince Charming." He pretends to leave, moving to grab his bag.

"Actually," he stops, "*Why are we* still meeting at shitty Starbucks when we could be doing this at Taylor's work? I'm going to text everyone and tell them to meet us there this morning. We're changing venue going forward."

He turns his back on us, hands flying across his phone at an alarming speed.

"He's frightening."

Rae smiles. "Tell me about it, imagine living with him. Come on, we best move before he causes a scene."

SETTLED IN AT CAFFEINE COMA, I listen on as Rae and Joanie argue over this month's pick.

"I don't read sci-fi, Joanie. Those were the rules, each of us placed a genre we weren't down with, and it was voted on. We *all* voted to oust the possibility of sci-fi."

Shaking her head, Joanie grumbles. "It was just a suggestion."

"When it's Tamra's turn to pick," Rae argues. "You do this every month. It's infuriating. Just wait your turn."

"That mohawk is draining blood flow from your brain, you're being exceptionally annoying."

Rae laughs. "It's my life goal, Joanie, annoying you."

Sighing, Joanie turns to me. "Is Rake single?"

Shocked at the sudden turn of conversation I open my mouth only to close it again. "Umm... I actually don't know."

Eyebrows pulled together, Joanie frowns at me.

"I know he's not married," I save myself the embarrassment of knowing next to nothing about my employer. "But he's never mentioned a partner."

Nodding her head, Joanie stands. "Good, I'm going to ask him out, excuse me."

"That chick is whack," Rae grits when Joanie is out of earshot.

"You know she does it to rile you up?" Tamra murmurs.

Shrugging, Rae refuses to meet her eyes.

From my limited interaction with Tamra, I like her, she seems nice. But the hot and cold she blasts Rae's way never sits right with me. I can understand being uncertain of your feelings, shit, I'm kind of an expert at it. But seeing it happen to someone I now classify as a friend, seeing first-hand the pain it causes, I regret even making anyone feel that way.

"Helllloooo, lov*ahhh*." Dex taps my knee, looking at the door.

I look up in time to see Tripp barge through, cell stuck to his ear, a look of irritation aging his face.

"That's Taylor's guy," Rae responds to Dex's drooling.

I'm too stuck on the tension radiating off Tripp to speak. I've seen him challenging before, a little argumentative, but never hostile. Never bristling with barely restrained anger.

Pulling his cell from his ear, he gives Rake his order, his attention moving straight back to his phone call as he pushes a bill across the counter. Waiting impatiently, he checks his watch multiple times, standing a good three feet from the rest of the customers, back aimed at the shop. His call ends only to have his hands begin a furious attack on the keys as he texts or emails.

Without thinking, I stand, moving toward him cautiously. Tapping his shoulder, he stuffs his cell in his pocket, turning quickly.

"Dove," he whispers, his shoulders deflating on an exaggerated breath. "God, it's nice to see you."

He pauses for a split second of time before stepping closer. "Can I kiss you? *Please?*"

"Umm..." I stutter, shocked at the tender need in his voice. "Okay."

His eyes close in relief, his large hands coming up to cup my cheeks and I barely have time to breathe before his lips are on mine. His kiss is *exactly* like him. Confident, gentle, passionate. *Addictive.* The softness of his lips brush mine with eagerness, letting the touch of my mouth ease him. The tip of my tongue darts out to taste his lips, a soft groan escaping his mouth, forcing me closer. The tender slide of his tongue against mine is like nothing I can recall ever feeling. Tripp Tanner is offering everything with this kiss, making me feel wanted, cherished and needed all at once.

Pulling away, his eyes flutter open, the color of liquid

silver hidden under heavy lids. Leaning in, his lips graze my ear. "See, dove, *magic.*"

Ducking my head, I work to hide both my smile and the likely shade of pink staining my cheeks.

Knuckle at my chin, Tripp lifts my face. "You have no idea how much that smile makes my day."

I wet my lips, savoring his taste. Seeing the move, he drops his lips to mine again, this time a quick touch of his lips before he pulls away. He steps over to the counter, retrieving his coffee on a wink of thanks to Rake.

"You working today?"

"No," I answer, pointing toward the corner where the entirety of my book club are gawking. "Book club, Dex made the decision that we needed a venue change."

"Smart guy. I'd love to stay, crash your party, but I have so much shit going on at work. A case I've been working on is falling apart around me, but I'd love to meet your friends?"

Unable to hide my smile, I nod. "I'd like that."

He follows me over to the group, my hand grasped in his.

Rae is the first to speak. "Tripp, nice to see you again."

He waves to Rae, refusing to let go of my hand.

I point through the group. "Dex, Joanie, Tamra, her sister Rose, Vera, and Quinn. Everybody this is, Tripp Tanner, my..."

"Boyfriend," he answers for me, squeezing my hand as his face drops to look at mine.

Eyes widening in shock, he winks at me.

"It was lovely to meet you all." He ignores my shock. "I wish I could stay, see my book club competition, but I've got to get to work."

Leaning down, his lips touch my ear. "About to kiss you again."

His lips are on mine before I can get a handle on his words, this time a soft brush of his lips against mine. "I'll call you tonight, dove."

And with that, he's gone, glancing back one last time to smile at me before disappearing through the door.

"You are a fucking magician," Dex whines. "Did you see his mood when he stormed through the door, then he sees you, *kisses* you and you sucked the angry right out of him. Teach me."

I laugh nervously. "I didn't do anything."

"Didn't need to, babe," Rae winks. "You calm him in the same way he brings you to life. Dex is right, it's like magic."

FOURTEEN

Had you told me four years ago that I'd be sitting in a room, *alone*, with a man, I would've been convinced of your insanity. My fear was a cancer within my soul, poisoning my mind, buckling my self-worth. The belief in my own safety was hijacked by the malignant blood flowing freely through my veins. But Tripp was his own form of radiation, slaying the enmity murdering me from the inside out. He eases me into comfort, into safety with the balm in his spirit. In his presence, I never feel as though I'm in peril. He's a safety net, a security blanket; one that alleviates my fears, both unknown and recognized.

Since our first date, we've spent countless hours in only one another's company. It feels good, knowing it's just he and I. Separated from the harsh distractions of our worlds. It's more freeing than I ever imagined it could be. I'm at peace in his company, which is more than I can say for my own most of the time.

Shifting on my couch, I clear my throat, feeling my dinner heavy in my stomach. We've spent the last few hours at my apartment, Tripp having cooked for me. The seafood paella was like an explosion of taste in my mouth, but now it feels like lead in my gut, twisting with the secrets of my past, making me want to vomit.

Our relationship is progressing, but I know I'm holding back. I've had to. How can I give him all of me when such a significant slice of my past is festering like a dirty secret?

I want him to know me. *All* of me, which includes all of the haunted and sullied shades.

"I want to share something with you," I speak, looking to my feet.

He hears the mumbled garble of my words well enough. "I'd love to hear it, but I need you to look at me. Whatever it is, I'm certain it's not deserving of the shame forcing you to hide away from me."

Inhaling heavily, I coerce my head upward.

"Why do you call me dove?" I ask.

Sliding his wine onto the table, he lifts the remote for the TV, switching it off as he twists his body, offering me his full attention.

"You think I'm pure? Innocent?" I test, panic rising in my voice.

"Can I hold your hand?" He shifts closer.

I glance down at my hand, watching it shake, the racing beat of my heart overtaking me. I squeeze my fist together to stop the tremor. "It's shaking," I tell him.

"Exactly why I want to hold it," he answers easily. "I want you to know that I've got you. You never need to be afraid of talking to me. About anything."

I let go of the fist my hand is twisted into, frowning at the indents my fingernails have carved into my skin. Reaching out, I place my hand in his open palm, letting the warm touch of his hand around mine soothe the nerves rippling through my body like an unrelenting current.

"I call you dove because the moment I saw you I felt peaceful. Even with the turmoil flashing through your eyes. There was something about you that was contentedly trans-parent. You wore your pain for all to see, you weren't trying to be someone else and I found it endearing. I wouldn't say you were *innocent?* But, yes, there's a purity about you that I'm attracted to."

My eyes close in regret. I shouldn't have asked. I'd guess as much, but hearing him confirm that he's attracted to some-thing about me that isn't real is devastating. I'm falling for Tripp Tanner and I'm falling *hard.*

"I'm not pure," I profess. "I'm tainted."

He wants to speak, I see it in the twitch of his jaw. The strong line forcing it to stay closed. He's giving me this, my chance to speak.

"My body," I scratch out, the words bleeding in agony. "My mind, my heart." I tap my chest. "They're all desecrated."

"The semicolon."

"Huh?" I stammer.

"Behind your ear." He touches the same space on his own body. "I saw it the first day I came into the coffee shop."

"You did?" I breathe.

He nods. "I was standing by the girl that asked you about it. You'd just put your hair up," he reminisces. "You were so beautiful. I couldn't help but stare, I heard her comment on the tattoo and watch how wound-up it made you."

He was there. He saw the mark on my skin that represents the dawn of my life. The moment I chose to continue to live.

"You touch it when you're uncomfortable. Do you know that? When you feel out of your depth, your middle finger runs along the tattoo absently."

I do as he just said, my hand reaching up to the line of my hair, rubbing the small inked mark behind my ear.

"Then I touched you." His nostrils flare as he speaks, his hand held tightly in mine, damp with the nerves shrouding his words. "And the *fear* that held your eyes captive." He shakes his head. "I've never seen anything like it."

The heaviest of silence falls between us, the sharp pull of my breathing the only sound in the otherwise still space. Our gaze is locked, caught in the fire of our racing heartbeats, refusing to blink. Too captivated by the man before me. The man begging me with the pain in his eyes for me to continue. To share my story. To let him into my heart, as damaged and as cynical as it now is.

"There's such a stigma around suicide," I frown. "I thought about it, more often than I care to admit."

"I'd fallen down a hole so dark, no matter which direction I looked, there was no light, no promise of more than what I was living." I barely register the sound of my voice before the words are out there. Hanging between us like the hooded executioner, ready to swing his axe down and sever our relationship before it really began.

"But you fought..."

I shrug, my head nodding in agreement, although I'm not quite sure it's true. "I guess I did. I pulled myself up, sort of."

"Did you try..."

I shake my head before Tripp finishes his sentence.

"I couldn't. There was this force always keeping me from moving into that reality. I'd lost my purpose, my will. I guess my want to survive was stronger, even though I couldn't recognize it at the time."

"Was there a reason?"

The question wraps around my neck like a vise, clamping down so brutally I cough.

"You don't have to tell me," he offers honestly, a line of concern carved into his forehead.

"There was a man." I ignore his comment. "He was strong," I testify. "Stronger than me. Not that it really matters, I guess, his strength, he made certain my ability to fight back was thwarted."

I feel a sense of regained control. My secret will no longer be dirty. Something I'm attempting to hide. Instead, it'll be a chapter I choose to share. It may signal the end of a relationship I never in a million years imagined I wanted. But hiding this part of my life, this part of *me* would only do wrong to us both in the long run.

"It happened almost five years ago," I continue when he doesn't speak. "My best friend at the time, she *loved* to party." I cough out a laugh considering how we were ever close. We were polar opposites, in every way possible. When I think about it hard enough, I consider that it was a loyalty we felt obligated to honor, we'd been friends since we were kids. That's what you're supposed to do, isn't it? Keep your childhood friendships alive. "Anyway, we were out, and some asshole slipped something into my drink."

A look of understanding crosses his face and I feel the need to clarify. "That's not even the reason I don't drink," I laugh, the sound lacking any form of humor, instead it's dripping in animosity. "I've never really cared for alcohol. I was drinking fucking soda."

He doesn't seem perturbed by my swearing, as out of character as it is. My anger is evident, understandably.

"I was out of it." I shake my head, remembering how foggy my brain felt in that moment, how confused and disoriented I was. "People thought I was drunk." Lips pressed firmly together, I force a smile onto my face. I can feel the sadness in the gesture, the hopelessness in the action.

I shrug. "Most of the night is pretty hazy, but I still remember the way he smelt, the pressure of his body on top of mine. This person, this man..." My stare has moved off of Tripp, settling on the untouched white of my lounge room wall. A blank canvas to replay my assault like the most haunting of movies. "*This stranger*..." I gulp. "I asked him to stop, I *begged* him to stop. I fought... as hard as I could anyway, but my body was *heavy*," I recollect. "I couldn't move," I recall my panic. "He hurt me, threatened me, he forced himself into my body and I was too weak to fight him off."

Squeezing my hand, Tripp pulls my attention, and I give him what he wants.

"I don't really want to talk too much about that night, about what happened. I hope you can appreciate that," I postulate. "Really, you know everything that you need to."

I wait for a sign of acknowledgment, one he offers with a quick nod of his head.

"I was in a *dark* place after it happened, through the trial, through his sentencing. In the end, I wanted *it* to end. The memories." I squeeze my eyes shut. "The self-blame, the hurt... I wanted to go to sleep and never wake up. At least that way I'd forever be safe. No one could hurt me again if I ceased to exist."

Lips pressed in a firm line, Tripp's face is scarily passive, but his eyes, they're swirling with barely restrained emotion. Swimming in glassy pools, his anger, pain, and need to protect shine brightly my way.

"I got this tattoo" —I rub the spot behind my ear— "as a reminder of the moment I chose me. My life may not seem poetic and full, but it's enough for me. I survived and this life I'm living is a testament to that."

Teeth biting into his bottom lip, Tripp coughs, clearing the dryness in his throat. "Only ever want you to feel safe, Taylor. To feel comfortable with who you are, in who I am, and what we share. Ever a moment you don't feel that, I need you to tell me."

It's amazing the difference age can make. Brady and I were still kids when I was assaulted, barely into our twenties when our lives changed forever. His reaction was driven by anger, by fury. He was sullen and bitter, fantasizing endlessly about killing the man who took something from us. Not me. *Us.* Brady was so caught up in his own helplessness, he forgot about me. His incessant need for revenge only made my grieving process harder. I was working to put everything behind me, and he sat happily in his rage, keeping me hostage, whether he knew it or not. Every trigger, every nightmare, every flinch against his touch would spike the vehemence inside of him. He'd rant, he'd throw things, he'd punch walls, he'd cry.

We were a mess. I couldn't comfort him. I couldn't *touch* him. I could barely speak about that night, let alone work to reassure him. What could I promise him? That we'd be okay?

That we'd get through it. Pfft. I didn't believe that. Not for a second. Nor did Brady. We stayed in that toxic bubble for too long because we didn't know any better.

Brady didn't want to leave me for fear of how it would make him look, in the same way I didn't want to push him away making him a victim. We were caught, snared in the actions of someone else with no power to break free.

Tripp though, while I'm certain by the look in his eye contemplated a murderous thought or two, placed his entire focus on me, on how to make this work in a way that makes me comfortable. I wonder if he would've been this under-standing at twenty-six. More, I wonder if Brady would've had the ability to rationalize easier with more life experience.

"I hate that you've been through something so harrowing. I hate that I can't erase it for you. But I told you some time ago that I liked you, and I do. A lot. My feelings for you are growing in a way I can't seem to rein in, not that I care to," he smiles. "I can't tell you how much I appreciate you sharing that part of your life with me, I can only imagine how hard it is to think or talk about. I'm always going to be here, for what-ever you need. We take this relationship at a pace that you're comfortable with."

"Why continue to torture yourself?" I ask, contemplative curiosity in my tone.

Lips pursed in perplexity, his head tips to the side. "I don't know what you mean."

"Me," I clarify. "I'm broken, Tripp. Being with me would have to be the ultimate chore; managing each and every fragile part of me. It's relentless."

His face twists in a way I can't read. I can't tell if he's irri-tated, confused, or both.

"It's just..." I pause, inhaling deeply to calm my over-wrought nerves. "I'm already fractured and my feelings for you continue to grow in a way I can't control. I've spent *years* coiling myself up in barbed wire with the sole intention to deter anyone and everyone from getting close. My skin is spiked in hate and I've been content settling there. Well, I was... until I met you. Piece by meticulous piece, you're unraveling me."

"*Dove.*"

Holding my hands up, I stop him. "Please let me finish." I massage my forehead, collecting my thoughts once again. "It hurts," I admit. "With every strip of wire you pull from my shield, I have to meet every painful memory head on. Scary part is, as agonizing as that is... it feels better than I imagined." I smile sadly. "I thought it was my shield when in truth it was my own self-induced prison. You're freeing me from a sentence I was certain was lifelong, but at the same time, you leave me vulnerable."

"Love will do that."

"I'm scared," I confess quietly. "You have the ability to hurt me more than I imagined another man could. You've pieced my heart back together and I'm frightened beyond belief that you also now have the power to shatter it into irre-deemable pieces. You could destroy me, Tripp."

"You think I don't feel the same way?"

My head flies up, eyes widening in shock.

He laughs. "Love isn't just blind, it's blissfully ignorant. Culpably *imprudent*. People talk of fears in reference to the most improbable of circumstance. Sharks. Heights. Ghosts. The greatest fear we *should* hold is that of our own feelings." He shifts closer. "Taylor," he implores, my hand still grasped in his. "Love is the one thing we should fear most in this world. It has the ability to destroy. People give their *life* for it. They obsess over it, they let it *consume* them. You fear I'll break your heart in the same way I'm afraid I will."

I swallow the acid of his words.

"You admitted so much as well. You're afraid you're *too* broken to be loved, if there even is such a thing. You're afraid of hurting me as much as I'm fearful of the same."

Staring into his eyes, I consider he's right. I couldn't tell you what I'm more disturbed by; the thought that he'll break my heart, or that I'll break his.

"I'm not a stranger to love, I've been there twice before. I'm not lying when I tell you that you're the prettiest put together human I've ever come across. Gosh, dove. You see broken, I see impeccable. You've taken all your fractured parts and rebuilt. You're magnificent," he whispers. "You see imperfections, I see the greatest parts of who you are.

"Your hesitance, your discomfort around people, the slow and measured approach you take to life. I find it endearing. I see it and it shines so brightly... your quiet strength. I've said it before, dove. You're the loudest thing I've ever seen, and I want to hear it all."

Opening my mouth to speak, he cuts me off with a quick shake of his head. "All I'm asking is to stop putting up walls. I'm invested in *this,* I think you want to be too. Sure, we could both get hurt. Horribly, painfully. But we could also fall into a form of love neither of us has ever felt before. We could experience the very best of what love and life can offer, and we could live that happily ever after for the rest of our lives."

Caught in the intensity of his stare, I sit quietly, not trusting myself to speak.

"I know which path I want to gamble on," he confesses, shifting onto his knees in front of me. "I'd choose happily ever after with you every time, dove. Every fucking time."

My chin wobbles, my head dropping to hide the quiver of my lips.

Forefinger cupping my chin, Tripp lifts my head. "Hoping you think I'm worth the same gamble."

"What if you begin to resent it? My hesitation, my need to pause... what if you begin to resent *me?*"

"You're kidding, right?" he splutters. "You need to look harder, *see* me better. It's my most favorite thing about you."

The solicitation in his voice is impossible to ignore.

"What?" I splutter in disbelief, still choosing to refute the truth in his tone.

He laughs. "It's like experiencing everything for the first time again and again. Our first kiss erased *every* one before it." The way he speaks is unlike anything I've heard before. The longing, the desire in the way he articulates his feelings. It's too much and not enough all at the same time. I feel over-whelmed by the earnestness in each and every declaration, but I never want him to stop. He's tender without being trite and without even knowing it, he's threading my heart back together in the shape of him.

"I know it wasn't a first for either of us," he continues. "But the build-up, the road we took to get there... it might not have been our first, but damn anyone that tries to tell me it wasn't the most important kiss I've ever given, that I've ever received."

He blinks, letting himself pause for a brief second to swallow the lump of emotion that cracks along his vocal cords. "Every moment I share with you is like that. The past no longer exists. You and I are living our world of firsts. It's exhilarating. It's freeing. It's fucking *magic*."

I nod, too afraid to speak, feeling everything that he says deep in my soul.

"Sometimes..." I clear my throat. "I can settle in a pretty dark place inside of my head," I admit. "Dark enough that I lose my way."

He smiles. "Lucky this here" —he points at my heart— "calls to me in a way that's impossible to ignore. Trust that as dark as you go, I'll always find you, bring you back."

"I'm gonna kiss you now," I tell him, my voice bound with the tears in my eyes.

Tongue tracking out to moisten the tempting line of his lips, he grins. "And I'm gonna kiss you back, dove."

FIFTEEN

Hands cupping his face, I pull him forward and he comes without complaint. He lets my lips brush against his, but unlike his promise, he doesn't kiss me back. Not straight away. Instead, he lets me kiss him. My lips moving over his in tender caresses.

With every drag of my lips against his, my need for more escalates.

I want him to kiss me back.

I *need* him to kiss me back.

But eyes closed, and with just an uptick in his breathing, he gives me nothing more.

Pulling back, I bring him into focus, the desperate pants of my breath echoing with his.

"You said you'd kiss me back."

"I did," he admits. The thick line of his Adam's apple bobs up and down. "Hanging by a thread here, dove. I so badly want to touch you, but I don't want to push you."

"Touch me," I combat desperately. "*Please.*"

Hands rubbing roughly down his face, he groans quietly, the violent need in the sound making me shift on the spot.

"Move closer to the edge." There's a softness to his tone, a quiet coax that tells me I'm safe. That he won't hurt me.

I shift along the couch, stopping as my butt rests against the edge.

Sitting on his heels before me, his eyes skate over my face, over my body. A lazy smile pulls at his lips, the lids of his eyes hooded in appreciation. Teeth skating over his bottom lip, he pulls at it, the skin whitening with his bite.

"You're in charge, dove. You say go, *we* go. You say stop and we fucking stop."

"Okay," I murmur, the anticipation of him touching me almost too much.

"I'm gonna kiss you now."

"Okay," I repeat, making him smile.

Raising up, his large hands bracket me, pushed into the couch at my sides. He doesn't touch me, not with his hands. Not yet.

His eyes, his breath though, they bathe me in his lust. The hooded gaze honed solely on me. His breaths; short and sharp, nostrils flaring slowly with every shuddered exhale.

His arms are rigid in their positioning, like marble, unmovable. The muscles of his biceps protruding heavily, the veins along his arms thick and visible. They're strong. Stronger than me, but I'm not put off by it, not with Tripp. Instead, I let my gaze run over them in favor, my own hands itching to move, to touch him.

"Things you need to remember." His whispered words kiss my lips, so close I could taste him if I wanted.

"You never have to ask permission to touch *me*. That clearance is yours without condition."

Starting at his wrists, my palms meet the soft warmth of his skin. Lifting my gaze, I settle it upon his, letting my hands drift upward, feeling him as I go. His eyes track over my face over and over again in a slow and steady rhythm of affection.

"Second, *this,* what we're doing, is supposed to feel good, *better* than. Any point it feels anything *other* than that, you tell me, and we put our brakes on."

"Brakes on," I echo. "Got it."

"You're driving, dove, keep hold of that." Leaning forward, his tongue darts out, the tip flicking my top lip, tasting me.

My mouth opens at his silent instruction. Lips delicately ajar, I wait, eyes open, focused on his. Closing the distance between us, my hands gripped to his biceps, Tripp kisses me. Lips cushioning mine as he brushes a gentle kiss against my top lip, then my bottom.

Third time, I kiss him back. My hands tighten their grip, pulling him closer and he comes without issue, his chest only a breath from my own.

I forgot how nice this was. *Kissing.* The simple intimacy that can fire every nerve ending in your body.

The simple feeling that winds its way around the most potent parts of who you are. Your heart, your mind, that pull deep in your stomach, pushing lower with every second that passes, making you want things you'd long since sworn away from.

His lips are soft, bruising without being brash. Dominant without being suffocating. His tongue dances with mine and I eagerly let myself get caught up in his melody. I let myself savor his taste. The promise of a tomorrow I'd long since forgotten about. Like an intoxicating mix of the smell of a spring rainstorm teamed with the luscious bite of the first hints of the summer sun. Everything you'd been waiting for.

Inching back, his tongue licks at my lips. "Grab my wrist," he instructs.

I swallow.

Head tipping to the side, his lips skate along the line of my jaw.

"I'm gonna touch you." He nibbles my neck.

I moan, barely conscious of myself as a person as I arch my neck farther, wanting him to continue.

"Don't let go of my hand. Who's driving, dove?"

Fingertips trailing the line of my thigh, my breath catches. "*M-e.*"

"Good girl," he groans, our hands moving under the hem of my skirt, inching along the soft skin of my thigh in a tender brush.

Pulling from my neck, I want to cry at the loss of his lips, but the intensity of his eyes, the potency in his stare makes me cry in a whole other way.

Liquid pools of blue watch me as his fingers hit their destination, skimming the apex of my thighs in the most tentative of touches.

A shuddered breath catches along my vocal cords, making him smile. "Feel good?"

I don't trust myself with words, don't trust my voice. I nod, the movement as wobbly as it is vigorous.

"Eyes on me." The words are a command, there's no doubting that. But he speaks them as though I'm the cracked piece of glass ready to shatter into a million and one pieces. I wanna tell him no, on the contrary, I *was* shattered glass, broken in a way I was positive was irreversible, but he's working to glue each and every fragmented piece back together.

Tripp Tanner is making me whole again and he likely has no fucking idea.

I do as he says, my eyes trained on him and only him. It's just us. The ugliness of my past is so far out of reach I feel like I'm floating. The higher I soar, the easier the pain falls away.

His caress fills the empty caverns of my soul. Not because of what we're doing, it's the *way* in which he touches me. The tentative command in his eyes holding me hostage. He's refusing to let me see anything, anyone but him.

The affection in his gaze soothes the rigid and bleeding wounds of my spirit. Something I thought I'd laid to rest *years* ago. Like a match, he's struck, and the part of me that made me *me* has ignited. The flame is small, but it's there, gaining momentum with every beautiful and torturous flash in his eyes.

"I'm about to slide my fingers inside," he hums. "Any point you want me to stop, you pull on my wrist."

My legs open farther in invitation.

It's all together shocking and startling at how freeing sharing my story with him was. I felt for sure we'd both need time to decompress. To come to terms with the trauma of my past, more the lasting effect it will likely have on any relationship moving forward. On the contrary, it's magnetized our attraction in a way I couldn't ever have anticipated. Tripp's understanding, his want to continue exploring what we share, knowing how difficult the road may be; it's pushed me deeper into my feelings, and strangely enough, I feel safer than ever.

The tip of his thumb trails the side of my underwear, a teasing touch to test my boundaries. I swallow, eyes still locked together, not blinking, our lips but a breath apart.

Confident with my reaction, Tripp's thumb edges underneath the fabric, flirting with the soft skin of my body that hasn't been touched by another person in almost five years.

I whimper, making his nostrils flare in appreciation.

He groans, eyes blinking shut briefly exaggerating the sound. "You're wet, dove." His thumb circles my entrance before sliding upward and repeating the action over my clit. His touch is slight, not quite ghosting but tender enough to make my back arch. The calloused pad of his thumb continues its smooth assault; up and down, small circles painted along my damp flesh.

"More?" He licks his lips.

I stutter around a soft *yes*.

"You feel good, baby." He smirks.

Shifting closer, his free hand lifts from its place on the couch to reach under my skirt. Fingers brushing against my swollen core as he pulls my panties completely to the side making me gasp; the sound whispered across his lips in a shock. My hand still wrapped delicately around his wrist, our arms twist, two thick fingers massaging my entrance before sliding effortlessly inside.

I'm shocked at how simple yet empowering my hand attached to his feels. Tripp is strong, he's imposing, there's no denying he'd be able to overpower me with limited struggle. Yet, I'm not afraid. This simple action of my hand *directing* his has gifted me a sense of power that I haven't felt in *years*.

My legs widen farther, a reflex of my body adjusting to his intrusion. I feel full, stretched in a way I haven't felt in years.

"You're so full with just my fingers," he rumbles, pleasure coursing over his features and dripping along his words in rough and barely restrained need. "Hot and soft, and so fucking wet."

My hand moves without instruction, pulling him farther into my body and he groans, head falling against my chest.

Head pulling back as quick as it fell, he gives me his eyes once again, shaking his head at the small smirk pulling at the corner of my lips.

"She's naughty too," he hums.

The shade of his eyes darken as his fingers curve upward, rubbing along the spot inside of my body that makes my eyes roll back in bliss.

A fiery silver gaze watches my pleasure. I've never experienced something with such great intensity before. The eye contact. It's violent and lazy. Lids hooded in desire, but the look like fire; flashing with heat. He holds me captive with that look, making certain I have nowhere else to go but with him. I can't look away, even as the buzz of my body intensifies. My eyes will to close, to give in to my pleasure, my hand itching to let go of his. To fist, to pull at my hair, to touch my breasts, to touch *him*. The demand in his eyes disallows it though, and I'm both turned on and grateful.

Tripp Tanner is giving me back my body with the command in his gaze. I'm confused, elated and deliciously numb all at once.

Palm pushed against my oversensitive clit, the tip of Tripp's tongue darts out to lick my bottom lip. Breath catching, my body rolls forward, needing, *wanting* more.

"*Throbbing*, dove," he muses. "Ready to come?"

I feel as though I've been electrified by his words. My entire body convulsing at the intimate teasing in his tone.

"*Yes,*" I whimper.

"Grind, baby," he urges.

My breathing stutters, but I do as he commands, my hips rolling to push myself heavier against his hand. His long fingers continue their ministrations inside of me; slowly massaging, rubbing soft and hard circles.

My mouth opens to speak, to groan, to cry but the sound cuts off at the base of my throat, coming out in a strangled sound of sex and surrender.

"That's it," Tripp growls. "Use me, dove. Fuck my fingers. *Harder,*" he demands.

My heart flutters in my chest, eyes begging to close, to give over to my pleasure, but I couldn't look away if I tried. The power in the deep pools of his eyes is greater than my need right now. He's determined to give this to me, to let me lose myself in the feeling coursing through my veins, his eyes anchoring me to my pleasure. I know, without testing the theory, that if I gave in, my lids closing to reach my peak, the intensity of my orgasm would be lost, the nightmares of my memories gaining access twisting this moment into something dark.

Rocking my hips forcefully against his palm, my hand on his wrist pulls tight. I pause, my body stilled into shock as my orgasm rips through me. Mouth opening, my silent scream kisses his lips, back bending in to arch back almost immediately.

A growl, anything but tender steals along my skin like a kiss he's yet to offer. Rippling across my flesh, raising it in its wake.

Chest expanding heavily with the thick breaths bursting in and out of my lungs, I glance at Tripp through my lashes, the cocksure grin pulling along the right side of his mouth sending flutters down my spine and right to where his hand is still connected to my body once again.

Still not breaking eye contact, he draws his fingers from my body. I whimper, hand tightening around his wrist in dispute. A silent chuckle moves his shoulders up and down.

I feel myself tighten as he leaves my body, a dull ache at the loss echoing through me.

Hand lifting, mine still attached, he brushes a finger across my parted lips. The salty taste of my release teasing my tongue as it darts out to taste. Pulling back, he watches me, his fingers finding his own mouth, lips closing around them.

He retracts them slowly. The move giving insight into what type of lover he'd be. Sensual, lavishly vulgar. The kind you crave. Caring enough to place your pleasure above his, still dirty enough to get you there.

A beat passes.

A moment.

Passed without a breath drawn.

All before our lips slam together, a kiss, fueled by desire, by relief, by a level of emotion neither one of us can comprehend spiraling around us like a tornado. Hands in my hair, Tripp lifts up, his chest crashing against mine.

Groaning into my mouth, the velvet slide of his tongue slides against mine.

Tripp was right, every time we touch, it's like a first. The moment so profound, every *before* washes away, offering a clean slate. Just us. No pasts. No tainted memories. No expectations.

Pulling from our kiss on a rough grunt, Tripp licks his lips. His mouth opens, but reconsidering his need to speak he kisses me instead. A quick, hard push of his lips against mine. Once, twice, three times.

"I can't stop," he laughs. "You're fucking delicious."

Pushing his face away, I chuckle.

"Wanna watch a movie?" he asks.

Nodding, I stand. "You choose. I'm gonna make a cup of tea, want one?"

"Love a coffee."

Standing in the kitchen, my underwear damp with my first accompanied orgasm in almost *five* years, I consider the changes in myself over the last few months.

I know *Zoe Lincoln* may never return in the way I remember her. The impact of my life experience has irrevocably changed the fundamentals of who I am as a person. But there are pieces, fragments of the girl I used to be breaking through the walls I've spent the last few years hiding behind. I never imagined getting to this point, more *wanting* to be here. I was so hell-bent on pretending I was content in my bubble of numb, I'd forgotten the pleasures of life.

Friends.

Company.

Relationships.

I wouldn't say Tripp is the reason, but he's definitely a beacon of hope. Like Rae, like Dex. I'm finding my community again and for the first time in too long, I feel like I belong, like I'm not living a lie.

Wandering back into the lounge, mugs in hand, I smile at Tripp on my couch, Potter snuggled eagerly in his lap.

"Cool with Harry Potter?" He leans forward, retrieving the offered mug.

"I've created a monster," I tease, settling beside him.

My eyes on the screen, I sense Tripp's face on mine. Twisting my head, I raise an expectant brow.

"You okay, dove?"

I blink softly at the tenderness in his tone. "Yeah," I assure him. "Yeah, I am."

"Good," he murmurs, leaning down to kiss me once again.

SIXTEEN

"Zoe, that's a huge step. Not just the physicality of what you shared, but divulging your past to Tripp is a poignant moment."

I fiddle awkwardly with the loose thread of my sweater. "I didn't tell him my real name."

Hannah shrugs. "You've taken a major leap forward, it's not necessary to divulge everything before you're ready. You take it at your pace."

"Do you think he'll be mad?"

Readjusting her hair, she contemplates my question. "I can't foresee how any one person will react to anything. From the snippets you've told me about Tripp, he seems like an understanding guy."

"The only thing you've falsified, Zoe, is your name," she continues when I remain silent. "Everything else is real. Your name doesn't define who you are."

I sigh.

"The important thing is that you don't tell him before

you're ready. He's the first guy you've actually shown an interest in, *including* Brady, since the attack. Don't rush into anything, *more,* don't *be* pressured into something from an assumed expectation."

My head moves up and down, a quick acknowledgment of her words before I turn the conversation back. "I expected to *freak* out when he touched me," I confess. "Like I did with Brady."

"Why do you think you didn't?"

I hate it when she does this. Makes me answer the questions I'm positioning at her. Forcing me to work through the train wreck of my own brain. It's like a never-ending maze, roadblocks at every corner.

"A lot of time has passed," I consider.

"True," she ponders.

"But?" I question, hearing the disagreement in her tone.

"You tell me."

I tip my neck back, groaning outwardly, much to her amusement. Righting my neck, I stare at her.

"Think about it," she pushes.

Turning my gaze away from my computer screen, I flick through the pages of illustrations I've been working on.

"DID I WAKE YOU?" Brady *tests, a soft hesitance to his tone.*

I hate that, their need to tip-toe around me on eggshells, working their hardest not to startle me.

"No."

He sighs at the one-word response, dropping onto my bed near my feet. I shift them, pulling them closer to my body. He takes in the protective ball I've forced myself into, anger burning in his eyes.

"Never hurt you, ZZ."

I bite my lip to hold back the sob tickling the vocal cords in my throat. "I know," I croak out after a second, confident I can speak without my voice breaking.

I moved back in with my mom and dad after everything happened. That was almost three months ago.

I barely leave the room. It's safe here. In my space. No one can force me to talk about what happened. No one can look at me with pity or sympathy, or worse, blame. More, no one can hurt me here.

I eat to placate my mother. To ease the pain that creases around her eyes. She feels inept. Like it's her job to help me heal. Heal. What a joke. Physically I look fine. The bruises of his fingerprints on my neck have faded, but what everyone doesn't realize is they're imprinted for life. I can feel it. His hand. Wrapped tightly around the column of my neck, cutting off my air supply. The hopeless need to breathe at the mercy of a monster who enjoyed seeing me suffer. See, what people don't seem to realize is that on the inside I feel as though he doused me in acid. Forever changed, scarred without hope of restoration.

I quit my job. It's kind of hard for an employer to continue to pay you when you refuse to leave the house. It was easier this way.

I don't sleep. Not ever. Not if I can help it. Awake, I can force my thoughts away from dark brown eyes and his evil smile. I can pretend as though I've never felt the weight of him on me. Asleep, that's a different story. It's an open invitation to every horrible detail of that night. Haunting me, mocking me.

"Zee," Brady pushes, his hand coming to wrap around my ankle.

I yank it back as though I've been burned.

"Jesus, Zoe. Fucking talk to me. I love you, I just want to touch you, hold you, fucking be here. Stop pushing me away."

I duck my head to hide the tears he knows are there. The thick droplets falling onto my shirt in a heavy reminder of the storm I'm caught up in. "I'm sorry."

I'm doing that a lot of late. Apologizing. I don't even know what for. For reverting into myself, for not being better, for not working to put this... incident behind me. For it happening in the first place. For hating every single person around me. More, for hating myself.

"I've been reading," Brady starts, shifting closer. "A lot of sexual assault victims feel powerful after claiming their control back. Zoe, if we kissed, touched in some way and you could feel it was me..."

I swallow the bile that begins rushing up my throat, frowning at the taste it leaves in my mouth.

Is he serious?

"Do you love me?" he asks.

"Yes," I lie. Truth is, I love nothing anymore. All I see when I look around me are reminders of everything I've lost. Everything that was stolen from me.

I see black. I see hate. I see the promise of a life that I can no longer reach.

"I love you, too. I feel so helpless... if I could kill that motherfucker." He shakes his head, and again I find myself swallowing. This time my resentment.

It infuriates me. His need for revenge. For vengeance. It consumes him.

"I think of everything he's taken from us, from you, from me," he continues, oblivious to my bristling anger.

"Kiss me," I cut him off, not being able to stomach another second, another word of his rage.

He pauses, eyes widening in shock.

"Yeah?" he checks.

Heart racing in my chest, I nod, against every screaming protest in my body.

I'm shaking, and more than a little certain that this will end with the limited contents of my stomach decorating my boyfriend's face... but at least I would've tried.

Leaning over me, my heart no longer races in my chest, it seizes, completely. Shocked into stillness as fear courses through my veins.

It's stupid.

It's Brady. The man I've been dating for almost two years. The man I've promised my love to. We've shared countless kisses, a similar number of sexual experiences. But right here, at this moment, I feel cornered. He's a stranger, a man stronger than me forcing something that I don't want any part in.

"I WASN'T READY WITH BRADY," I resolve. "Nowhere close. I was also doing it to appease him... not because I wanted to."

Hannah smiles triumphantly.

"He was so considerate," I tell her. "Tripp was. He knew how easy it would be for me to slip into my memories. Once upon a time, *too* much eye contact during sex or intimacy of any kind would've weirded me out," I balk. "But Tripp, he seemed to know it was exactly what I needed to keep in the moment."

"He's older than Brady was," she defends. "Life experience, maturity, they offer a lot for understanding and empathy. A boy in his early twenties is starkly different in their approach to trauma to a man in his mid-to-late thirties. *Most* of the time anyway."

"I have a few fears," I admit. Readjusting the screen of my Mac, I lighten the screen, wanting to see Hannah better.

"What's first?"

Clearing my throat, I vocalize the easiest of my anxieties to identify. "That when the time comes that we move farther, that we attempt to have sex, I'll go into meltdown."

"Common placed fear," Hannah surmises. "Not unusual, not unexpected."

"How do I stop it from happening?" I beseech. My neck feels hot, the panic of my demand creeping up in a dread I can't shake.

"There's no magic cure, Zoe," she chides. "Don't try before you're ready, that's my first piece of advice."

Irritation blurs my vision. Not at her. Not even at myself. This whole situation is a disaster. One that makes me question why I'm even attempting any form of relationship.

"Second," she continues, her voice having dropped an octave. "Take it slow, the two of you jumped a massive hurdle, *together*. Tripp seems to understand the situation, if you freak out... *you freak out*." She shrugs. "It wouldn't be the end of the world."

I consider she's right.

"The scar." I touch it absentmindedly through my pants. A bite mark so brutal, the power of his jaw is still indented in my skin like a tattoo I never wanted. Ugly. Marred. Almost five years old, and it still hasn't healed; it's thick and tight and still psychologically raw. It's a reminder that wants to stay with me forever. A disfigured token of what I survived. "It's hideous."

"Scars aren't exactly pretty. Visible or not."

"What if he's repulsed?"

I watch her take a sip of water, her hand coming up to dry her lips as she considers her next words. "Would you be repulsed at seeing something similar on Tripp?"

"No," I combat immediately.

She raises an eyebrow. "So tell me why you think he'd feel any different."

I pause, not quite certain on how to respond.

"If Brady were standing in front of you right now," she continues. "What would he tell you... dig deep, Zoe. You spent two years of your life with him."

"He was mad when he saw it," I challenge.

"Was he repulsed? Disgusted? Show any sign of him not finding you physically attractive because of it?"

I turn my head, again unable to find words.

In truth, Brady was still one hundred percent physically attracted to me. He begged me to let him touch me. To share what we once had. A physical connection that ignited our emotional relationship. Sex brought us closer together, made us feel more connected. He craved that, craved *me* to the very end. Or so I think.

"Intrusive thoughts, Zoe. They only aim to mess with *your* mind. Remember the strategies you've learned to combat them."

"Easier said than done," I gripe.

"You're doing so well, Zoe. I understand how frustrating it must be to come up against roadblocks again and again but look at the progress you *have* made. You'll learn to manage your path back into sex like everything else."

"I'm falling for him," I whisper. "It seemed such a farfetched thought... even a few months ago. But I'm falling in love and I'm terrified. What if my feelings are real, but I can't scale *this* mountain? What if I can't find the passion sex should bring?"

She nods, completely understanding my fear. It makes me feel better, if only slightly. She wasn't in the least bit surprised by my trepidation, which makes me think it isn't the first time she's dealt with anxiety around this very issue.

"Sexual assault victims are all different. Some dive straight back into sexual encounters, using them as a coping mechanism, not always healthy, mind you, for their trauma."

Leaning toward the screen, her face changes. "Others *avoid.*" She doesn't need to say anything more to identify she's talking about me, maybe not specifically, but as a census. "They refrain from any and all kinds of sexual interaction, fearing the thoughts it could stir up."

"And," she adds, "others willingly participate sexually in a relationship, but with the sole purpose of satisfying their partner. They lack passion, they struggle to find their desire, their hunger for sex."

"No one is right in how they approach it, nor are they wrong. The journey is completely individual. You'll find your way."

I want to believe her. With every cracked and flawed crevice of my soul, I want to believe her. But I've spent *so* long believing in nothing, putting one foot delicately in front of the other, juggling the precious cliffs of this thing called life, I'm just not sure my cautious nature will let me give into the hope simmering within me.

"Here's the one thing you need to remember. *The* most important fact to keep with you always." She waits for my full attention. "Sex isn't just a physical activity, there's meaning behind it. Be it lust, love, *anger* even, it's an expression of a deeper feeling. The connection it brings is incomparable. Just because someone took liberty on something that should always be a declaration between two consenting adults, doesn't mean it has to forever remain that way. Sex is fun, Zoe. It's pleasure and feeling and expression. It's *connection.* A positive one."

"You deserve the intimacy, the pleasure, the enjoyment sex can bring. You're entitled to that as much as anyone. Once you remember that, it's yours to reclaim."

I remain silent, unsure how I want to respond.

"It's likely a concept you're not ready to grasp. But you will."

Rubbing my hands along my face, I growl out my frustration. "Damn Tripp Tanner and his ill-timed arrival in my life."

She frowns.

"What?" I question.

"What?" she responds.

"You're frowning."

She rubs her forehead. "Am I? It's just... Nothing." She dismisses me with a wave of her hand, sounding anything but content in her thoughts. "No time is ever perfect," she mumbles distractedly.

"Time's up," I offer carefully, a niggle of worry at her outward show of emotion throwing me off.

"It is," she agrees absently.

We end the call, the crease in her forehead still deep.

SEVENTEEN

I stare at my cell, nail caught between my teeth in indecision, Hannah's words echoing in my ear like an incessant mosquito, buzzing in promise.

If Brady were standing in front of you right now what would he tell you... dig deep, Zoe. You spent two years of your life with him.

"His number is probably different." I turn to Potter who pays me zero attention, too caught up in licking his paw.

"You're a terrible companion, you know that?" Again. Nothing.

Fucking cats. Maybe Rae is right. Maybe my cat is evil. I let myself watch him for a beat, turning away quickly when he looks up as to not let him catch me.

I've lost it. Officially.

I growl, massaging my temples.

Years have passed and I still remember his number. I don't know whether that's sad or impressive. I dialed it enough times after I ran away, wanting to hear his voice. The happy hitch in his tone. Truth is, after everything went down, that smile in his voice was as lost as we were. Brady was drowning like I was, and I knew he wouldn't make the decision to save himself.

The dial tone pounds against my eardrums and my whole body breaks out in goosebumps.

"Hello?"

I consider hanging up, the impact of his voice hitting like a freight train, every lost promise shooting through my body like electricity; both agonizing and therapeutic all at once.

"*Hello?*" he repeats.

"Brae," I scratch out.

Silence hangs on the other end and I pull the phone from my ear checking the connection.

"*Zoe?*"

"Yeah," I reply. The word is as wobbly as I feel, but I stand all the same, needing to move.

"Hi," I test after another pregnant pause.

"Hi," he breathes out. "Always hoped I wouldn't forget the sound of your voice, thief."

The soft endearment makes me smile. It makes me cry.

"How you doing, ZZ?"

My feet stop their movement, head tipped downward, jaw wired shut as I swallow back my tears. "I'm doing okay, Brae," I grit out. "Better every day."

I hear the break in his voice as he speaks. "Real fucking glad to hear that."

"Mom told me you got married," I offer, saving him the awkwardness of needing to divulge that himself.

"I did. You remember Kenzie from school days?"

I smile. "Yeah, I remember Kenzie. I like her for you."

He laughs quietly. "I like her for me too."

My feet begin their incessant pacing once again, only this time, it's not nerves or uncertainty propelling me forward.

"I was afraid you would've hung up on me," I confess.

I can see his face, clear as day. The thick line of his brow pulled in tight, face alight with confusion. "Why the fuck would I do that?"

"You'd have every right to hate me."

He sighs. "One, I got no right to hate you, and two, it's not possible."

"You told me once upon a time that if we ever stopped loving one another, you couldn't be my friend."

I hear him move, likely pacing his home, wherever that may be, similarly to me. I think it's where I picked up the habit, watching him for those years.

"That statement alludes to the fact that I stopped loving you."

That gives me pause and I suck in a sharp breath, shocked by his declaration.

"Calm down," he chuckles on the end of the line. "Different kinds of love, ZZ. I still love you," he implores. "Just not in the way that sees us lookin' at one another forever with hearts in our eyes. Doesn't mean you aren't an important piece of my heart. Always will be."

I swallow down the lump in my throat.

"How is Kenzie?"

The immediate change in his voice is impossible to miss, the pain giving way to the happiness his wife shrouds him in. "She's good. She's pregnant."

Gripping my jaw, I stop it shaking. "Brae..."

"I know," he whispers.

There's a pause in time where we let ourselves get lost in

the past. Remembering the future we'd planned for ourselves, the one he's now living with someone else. I take comfort in the quick intake of breath on his end of the line. I grind my teeth, working to stop the frail sob wanting to escape.

"Still grinding your teeth to stop that little mouse cry?"

I laugh, the sound mixing with my cry resulting in a rough hiccup.

"I'm not crying because I'm sad," I assure him. "I'm so happy for you, Brady. I thought... I know I hurt you. Badly."

"You did no such thing, Zoe. *No* such fucking thing," he spits. "Our relationship was the collateral damage in an internal war that piece of shit..." His voice breaks and closing my eyes I let my tears fall. "That piece of shit," he repeats. "Raged inside of you." He pauses. "Inside of me," he finishes regretfully.

A heavy silence sits on the line.

"You didn't hurt me, not really... you *saved* us," he urges. "You hadn't have ended us, ZZ, I would have stayed," he confesses.

"I know."

"Then you know if that happened, I would have ended up hurting you. Not on purpose, but... I would have drowned in my own helplessness. I would have stayed and *tried,* but I would've sought solace elsewhere, eventually. I hate even admitting that. God, it makes me sound like a piece of shit."

"Nothing wrong with searching for love if the person who's supposed to give it to you is purposely starving you of it, Brady."

"Yeah, there is, babe, when they're hurting through no fault of their own, there is something wrong with it."

He's matured a lot in the past few years. I'm sad that I missed it, but happy that he's found his peace all the same.

"We were kids, don't hate yourself for something you *think* you would've done."

He exhales heavily. "You breaking it off was the right thing. *You* were right, like always." He laughs, the sound clogged with emotion. "You needed to move away from this life, away from the memories you were suffocating in."

He doesn't vocalize his next fear, the one that kept him awake at night, the one that fired his anger in wanting me to *get better*.

I would've ended up hurting myself.

The demons in my mind were the strongest part of me for so long, I would've given in. He knows it. I know it.

Our ending ensured we both survived.

But that's life. Broken hearts happen. They heal, apparently. Maybe for some. Definitely for Brady. Maybe they're put back together a little differently. Likely a little bumpy with the life experience of heartbreak. The price of happiness, having your heart broken before you find that ending, the one surrounded in your forever love. At least that way you know what you have, enough to hold on hard enough when it's pushed to its limit.

"Brady?"

"I'm here."

"Thank you. For everything. For trying to hold on. For trying to make me see past the twisted knots of my heart. You didn't give up on me, even when I'd given up on myself. I'm sorry I've never said that before. I know I just... *ran*."

"You didn't run, thief, you chose to *live*, whether you knew it at the time or not. You'll see that one day. You changed your trajectory, you're a fucking warrior, Zoe Lincoln. Strongest one I know."

"I like that you see me that way."

He *hmphs*. "Just wish you'd finally see yourself that way."

"I met someone."

A beat of silence and I can *hear* his smile through the line. "That hurt a little more than I considered it would." He chuckles. "Bet he ain't good enough for you," he teases.

"He's somethin' all right," I murmur.

"You stealing breaths again."

I can't even find it in me to laugh again, the weight of what I was about to ask him as mortifying as it is inappropriate.

"ZZ," he calls. "You there?"

"Yeah, look, I shouldn't have called, I'm being stupid..."

"Zoe," he combats my rambling with a stony bite of my name. "You can talk to me about anything."

"Was I disgusting?" I blurt out. "When we... that time we... after..." I take a breath, working to calm the storm in my chest. "The scar," I clarify. "Was it repulsive?"

"Jesus fuck, Zoe. *No.* Did I do something to make you think that?"

I shake my head before realizing he can't see me. "No. I just, it's *so* ugly. How could you want to... you know—"

"Fuck you?" he cuts me off. "*Touch* you."

"Yeah."

"Not a day passes that I don't wanna kill that soul-sucking parasite," he grits out. "Zoe, I don't know how to tell you this in a way that you'll believe." He pauses and I drop to my couch, waiting. "The mark that oxygen thief left on your skin is the least fucking significant thing about you. We all have scars, ZZ. Visible or not, the ugliest ones are usually the ones none of us can see. The ones visible to the eye are just an insight into the shitstorm of our minds and trust me when I tell you, you ain't got nothing compared to some of the others I've seen. You standing there naked, Zoe, you're beautiful, fucking exquisite. That pretty face, your beautiful body, trust me when I tell you that indiscriminate mark doesn't even register. There's too much gold, no one's looking for the blemishes."

"I don't want him to be turned off..."

"He's turned off by that, I was right, he ain't worthy of you and you should turn your back faster than he does on you. You're beautiful, Zoe Lincoln, fuck I wish you could see that past the ugly he painted in your life."

"Thank you," I whisper.

"Anytime," he replies just as gently. "But also, my wife is standing next to me nodding her head, encouraging me to praise your body and it's all kinds of fucking weird."

I laugh. "Tell Kenzie I said hi. I should let you go. Thank you, Brady. It was nice talking to you. I missed your voice."

"Back at ya, kid. Don't leave it so long next time. You sound on your way to happy, ZZ. Not lying when I tell you that it's one of the few things I've ever asked for in this life."

I bite my lip to stop it from trembling. "Bye, Brady."

"Bye, Zoe."

EIGHTEEN

almost five years earlier

My head spins and as hard as I work to see properly, my eyes won't cooperate. My brain has been replaced by a bass drum within my skull. The thick strike of a mallet against the brittle bone. It feels ready to crack, ready to shatter.

My mouth is both barren and damp. Craving moisture as saliva multiplies at an alarming rate, my stomach heaving, throat constricting with the need to be sick. Every movement fires my want to dry retch, my body too weak, too feeble to cooperate. Instead, a pathetic gag of air replaces the act, heightening my despondency. My thoughts are no longer my own. My brain now a hostage, just like my body, screaming for safety while at the mercy of a man who cares very little at showing it to me.

"That's it, sweetheart, just through here."

The shapes of the room don't quite fit as mine, or Brady's for that matter.

"Wh—" My tongue feels heavy in my mouth, the words

balancing on the tip, lost against the mumble of confused syllables and spit.

"Shhhh," he placates.

I shrug away from him, stumbling into a wall causing him to swear.

"Oh, no you don't, back here."

I cry out at the force in which he grips my arm, but like my words, it tumbles out in a mess of garbled sounds. I hear him laugh, the sound anything but kind.

I have no idea where I am, worse than that, I have zero recollection of how I came to be here. I was with Ella and where the rest of the story should be, I see only black holes.

A hand moves to my head, gripping my hair roughly, pushing me forward. I fall, the soft burn of the carpet scraping my knees and palms.

"Get up," he demands, but I fall again, my body refusing to oblige the haze of my mind.

Up. I think the word over and over again. *Up.* As if the simple syllable will let me recall the ability to stand.

He sighs. "Fucking useless."

Rough hands grip my armpits and I grunt at the unforgiving way my body is dragged upward. My head spins, my vision blurring to a point of blindness just before my world turns black.

I'm wrenched back into consciousness with the burn of a backhand against my cheek, a sting slicing against my face in the harshest of wake up calls. My already altered vision blurs further, warping my assailant into multiple beings. I don't know where to focus.

The man speaks, continuously, barely taking a breath. My

ears feel hollow, bass drums echoing inside, cutting off my ability to hear. Certain words are clearer than others.

Bitch.

Slut.

Reject me.

He laughs a lot, embodying the joy he finds in my pain.

Is he teaching me a lesson about rejection? Forcefully lecturing me on power; more so, how little I have in comparison to him?

"*Please,*" I hear myself beg, the word stronger than I imagined it would.

"My pleasure." He grins, pushing my chest with such force I fly backward, landing on his bed with a thud.

I struggle to move, to back away, but he's always there. No matter which way I turn, he's there, perverting my space. He surrounds me. I can't escape. I'm caged in by my own body's incompetence. Trapped by his perfected capability.

I feel cold to the touch, a breeze-catching along my skin like a million needles. I'm naked, and I have no idea how I got that way. Tears like ice cut from my eyes, slicing along my temples in potent fear.

I can't determine whose body feels heavier; mine or his. The dead weight of my body is being swallowed by the mattress I've been tossed upon. My mind screams at me to move, to fight, but my limbs are like cinder blocks, overburdening my muscles. His body feels like a ton of water collapsing on top of me. Submerged and oppressed so heavily that fighting is futile.

I am weak. He is strong.

I close my eyes against the depressing nature of that thought, that no matter how hard I fight right now, which is feeble with the situation he's imposed upon me, he will win. An overwhelming need to be sick waves through me. He'll always win. Because he is strong, and I am weak.

Palm gripped bruisingly along my jaw, he shakes my head from side to side, bringing me back into a consciousness I'd prefer to desist. At least asleep I don't have to bear witness to my own surrender. I can remain unaware of the trauma he'll inflict on my heart and soul as he defiles my body.

But that would be too much to ask. He's enjoying watching from above as I beg. As I break. As I sorrowfully admit defeat.

"Please," I cry, my saliva clinging to my lips like thread, binding them together.

I attempt to buck him off, using every bit of power I can muster to throw my hips upward. A soft chuckle at my pathetic attempt.

Palm like acid, his touch burns around my neck. He squeezes, robbing me of my last liberty; *breath*. I attempt to swallow, to breathe, but I fail. Leaning down, the rancor of his words bite along my ear.

"I could kill you so easily," he muses, the threat more frightening with the joy in which it's delivered. "Come on, Zoe," he uses my name like we're well acquainted. "Maybe you'll enjoy it."

He slides his fingers against my flesh, feeling the entrance to my body on a soft groan. "Or not."

"HELP."

My scream echoes along the walls. I hear the girl shrieking. The terror built upon the brittle sound of her cry. It shatters my pounding heart. I wish I could help her. I wish I could rescue her from the torment she's so obviously caught in.

But I am her, and in this very moment, I hold *no* power. I can't help her. The girl screaming for someone to save her. Because laying inside of her is me; the broken soul, wings clipped, lying dormant within, ready to accept the worst moment in my life with the taste of my own defeat on my tongue.

The timbre of my screech angers him. His face turns red with fury, blotching along his cheekbones, chin, and neck like an unhealthy rash. Even in my groggy state, I wonder how I ever considered this man attractive. He's vile. From the black tar of his insides to his overly perfected facial features. He's the scariest of monsters, the malignant cancer in the soul of society.

He shifts, letting me breathe and I let hope fuel inside of me. The small kindle stirring in my stomach like my prayers have been answered.

Then his teeth rip into my inner thigh.

My mouth stretches open on an inaudible scream. My leg throbs in an agony I've never felt, tearing at my flesh making me feel as though my limb has been severed from my body. He continues to lock his jaw over my flesh for what feels like an eternity.

Kneeling over me, blood drips down his chin, staining his teeth like a real-life vampire. Tongue dragging along the straight blood streaked line, he snarls. "Next time it'll be your fucking neck."

I close my eyes as his hands move to the buckle of his jeans. It's at that moment the sound of the world drops away, and all that I'm left with is the anticipation as his belt is pulled from his waist, a quick *whoosh* of air before it falls to the carpet in time with the thump of my heart.

The sound of his zipper pinches every inch of my spine as it descends, and I lock still in fear. I thought I couldn't move before, my body too heavy to move. Now terror has me hostage, and aside from the epileptic shake racking through me, I feel as though I've been doused in cement. Forever embalmed in this horrific moment. Forever to be remembered, too brutal to forget.

People reflect on their near-death experiences in wonder. They talk of how their life flashes before their eyes. Their memories and loved ones coursing through their mind like a picture show.

Wanting to die is different, I reason, as he forces his way into my body, tearing open my insides. Concentrating so hard on wishing your heart would stop beating so you wouldn't have to endure the torture of his thrusts. I pray. I beg whoever will listen to end it, my life, steal my last breath so I never have to relive the torment of this moment ever again.

He grunts, and I consider that bleeding out slowly would be preferable.

His hand finds my naked breast, pinching at my nipple with a calloused caress and instead of wincing at the pain, I deliberate that having my body pierced by a bullet would be my wish.

I don't fight.

Not that I can, but even if my body chose this moment to come back to me, I'd remain still. Suffering through. Why bother fighting? The damage is done. The damage was done the moment he slipped something into my drink and took my choice away from me.

He demands I open my eyes. I ignore him. He slaps me, and *still*, I refute his request. His fingers press into the already bruised marks of my neck, cutting off my ability to breathe. If only he knew that was what I wanted, so *still* I disregard him.

In the end, I couldn't tell you what sound he made when he came, or if he spat any derogatory comments as he spilled his seed. He used a condom, I know that, I saw it discarded on the bed as he dragged me upward and told me to get dressed.

He watched me stumble as I hurried to pull my dress on with my body still like lead. Marginalized me like a one-night stand he couldn't get rid of, instead of a girl he'd just raped. Shoes shoved into my chest, he walks me to the door, to the elevator, his evil hand tipped at my lower back.

I walk like the living dead. One foot in front of the other, eyes cast downward, avoiding my surroundings like a plague. The elevator chimes, doors sliding open and before I can rush inside, he lifts my chin, kissing my lips.

"Forced pussy is always so much tighter," he whispers, stepping back.

He's drenched in an eerie confidence. Zero concern for the heinous act he just committed. He feels invincible, *untouchable*. Dressed only in a pair of lounge pants, my blood still clings to his chin like a trophy. I'm certain if I was brave enough to look down, my leg would look similar. Streaked with trails of red, tears caused by the imprint of this teeth decorating my skin in a morbid illustration.

Stepping into the elevator, I pay special attention to the linoleum flooring, afraid to look him directly in the eyes for fear I'll crumble. My breath lodges in my throat as the doors slide closed, and as they push together signifying my release from a monster I never imagined meeting, the dam breaks. The exhale is shaky, my mouth dropping open to let go of a wretched sob.

I'm cold. My body is trembling, but I can't be certain that has anything to do with the ice clinging to my skin. It could very well be a symptom of the death of my heart, warm blood no longer being pumped through my body, instead guilt and regret spikes through my veins, leaving me cold and empty. Tears fall along my cheeks in a silent stream. I don't attempt to remove them. What would be the point? Their replacement would fall less than a second later.

I limp through the lobby of the building, paying no mind to the judgmental glances being tossed my way. I know how I must look. Creeping from an apartment that isn't my own, my skin like a beacon of shame, shining with the intense feeling. They can't know the origin of my disgrace. They look at me like I'm dirty and they're not wrong. They see me stumble, reconciling it as the effects of a night out that went too far. Again, they're not wrong. I look like the aftermath of a one-night stand and they judge me for it. How would they know the truth? Head ducked, they can't see my tears, they can't see the panic I feel that someone might approach me, opening the floodgates to my emotions. They see a girl tarnishing the opulence of their lobby with her filth and *again* they're not wrong.

I couldn't tell you how long I was with him for, but as I step through the threshold of the building, the effects of whatever he gave me waning with every minute, the bright greeting of the morning hits my face with a light that had abandoned me in my time of need.

My cab ride is quiet. I don't know if the driver notices my mental state. The way I need to pull my hands tightly against my chest to stop them visibly quaking.

"This it?"

My head remains downcast, hearing, seeing nothing.

"Honey." The cabbie speaks louder, forcing my head up. "This it?" He gestures out the window, and I follow his direction.

Mine and Brady's apartment building sits like it always does. Like nothing has changed.

I nod, hand rummaging in my bag, I throw a handful of cash in the driver's direction, shuffling out of the cab quickly.

The trudge up the stairs is painful. My leg aches, it pulsates in pain, and I pause, holding the wound only to feel fresh blood wet my dress.

After what feels like an eternity, I reach my door. Pushing it open, I do so slowly, quietly, hoping like hell Brady is still sleeping.

Back against the door, I slide to the ground, the back of my head hitting the door on a thud that shakes my skull.

I hear his feet, the slam of his footsteps against the wood of our hallway.

"Zoe, where the fu—"

His words stop abruptly.

His worried eyes scan my face, graze over my body in panic. "What happened?"

The way he rushes to my side, the break in his voice as he sees me, it's my undoing. A show of kindness to magnify the cruelty I have just endured.

I shatter.

Beyond recognition.

A cracked open shell of the person I used to be.

Before no longer exists.

It's all *after*.

And after is a poisonous abyss I'm free floating in, waiting to die.

I shift out of his touch when he moves to hold me.

I yank my hand away as though he's fire when he attempts to take it.

Curled into a ball as small as I can manage, I build an impenetrable forcefield around myself, denying him entry.

"Zoe, who the fuck did this?"

"I don't know," I stutter out around soul-shattering whimpers.

"Did... Did he?" His words are spoken so softly, the fear in them so potent, I can hear the crack of his heart echo against them.

I squeeze my eyes shut, unable to vocalize a single syllable.

"*Baby,*" he breathes out, falling to his ass with impact. Before he's settled into the jolt of my revelation, he scurries to his feet.

"We gotta call the police."

"No," I attempt to argue, my voice unheard over his determination. "No," I repeat, and he stops.

"I heard you the first time." He punches numbers into his cell, staring down at me, eyes wide with fury. "But there is no fucking way you're gonna let a piece of shit get away with this, Zoe. He... *he...*"

"I know what he did," I grit out. "I was there." My chin wobbles and I bite my lip, holding my jaw in place. "I want to forget it, I don't want to..." My words trail off, pleading with him to understand.

Crouching down in front of me, he genially keeps his distance. It's like the world has cracked down the middle, the gap widening with the earthquake of my *after*. Me left on one side, *alone;* the world safe and protected on the other.

"You're in shock," he offers. "Zoe, if this was anyone else, you'd want the piece of scum to suffer. You'd want justice for them."

He's right. One hundred percent. If it were any of my friends sitting where I am, and I where he is, I'd be vomiting the same spiel. I can't deny that, so I don't.

"What if he's done it before? What if he does it again?" he prays on my conscience, and I hate him for it. "The scum needs to be locked away."

Lowering my eyelids, I nod. "I don't even remember... I don't know."

"That's fine," he placates. "Let's just start with a call to the police and then we need to get you to a hospital. Let's get you fixed up."

Fixed up.

I want to laugh at how absurd that comment is. Brady likely doesn't recognize what he's just said. I want to pull him back here and tell him I'm irrevocably broken. That he needs to understand being *fixed* will never be a possibility. But his voice echoes around the apartment as he speaks into his cell, the words that will now define me wrapping around me like *his* hand did my throat.

"My girlfriend's been raped."

NINETEEN

I wake with a start, bed sheets twisted around my body, stuck with the glue of my sweat, binding me in place. My breath sounds like I've run a marathon. The laborious rhythm heaving my body in melody. Untangling myself in irritation, I peel my sheets from my skin, throwing them along my mattress in easy dismissal.

Feet planted on the floor, I inhale deeply, elbows to knees to calm my overwrought emotions. I never imagined you could shake on the inside. Your nerves so brittle they quiver under your skin. It's almost worse. Limbs you can hold onto, pause them in their need to tremor, but you have zero power over what stirs within you. I guess that's a poetic truth. Our hearts feel what they will, no matter how hard we plead with them. Our mind is the same; you can meditate. You can center your thoughts. But it doesn't mean you hold absolute power. Your mind will wander where it may. Only the strongest of people, or maybe it's those with nothing to lose who can shut it down, turn it off like a humanity switch.

I'm so tired of being caught in my head. Of fearing the

world as much as I do my own thoughts and memories. I *hate* that I've let one pinnacle moment define the life I'm living. My *after* is an ode to Miller Jacobs and I'm *so* angry at myself for handing that to him without a fight.

He's taken so much from me. *Much more* than I was ever willing to give. My body, my choice was one thing. But my family, my home, my relationships. I fell so hard down a dark hole of misery, I let myself wallow there.

I needed something to remind me of what life was about. Of what I was *missing*. Hannah was right, as soon as I dipped my toe back into the world, I found it. I found *them*.

Rae. Tripp. Dex. Rake. Hannah, even though she'd give me a stern look for considering her a friend.

I can walk into a foreign space and not count how many steps it will take me to escape.

I can converse with people and not completely fall into myself when they challenge me.

I've welcomed strangers into my home, into my safe haven.

I've been on a date.

I've been *kissed, touched*.

And I survived.

More, I fucking embraced it, I enjoyed it. I *lived* it.

Nightmares like what just woke me are becoming less frequent. They no longer force me into a ball, unable to move for fear they'll reappear.

I get up, yeah, I'm shaky. But I. Get. Up.

I persevere.

Because I'm a warrior.

My fingers reach for my tattoo, rubbing the spot with affection.

A survivor.

I stand, ignoring the pounding in my heart. Searching for my cell, I step over Potter, currently crossing through my feet working for attention.

"Oh, now you want attention. Have I ever told you that you're a terrible companion?"

My fingers fly across my screen.

Dove: Breakfast?

Tripp: See, I am magic. I thought this. It happened. I can see the future.

Dove: I make a mean frittata if you want to come to my place.

Tripp: Now if I could only work out that whole teleportation thing... Be there in 30?

Dove: Perfect.

Tripp: You're perfect. I still can't teleport.

I'm pretty sure I love him. It's the only justification for the stupid smile on my face. The only rationalization for the way my heart stutters at how often he crawls into my thoughts. I miss him the moment I leave him, mourning the loss of his presence at my side. He makes me laugh in a way that I'd forgotten I could do. He challenges me; pushing me to step out of my numb zone and I'm shocked to admit that I enjoy it.

I feel ready to live, and I feel ready to live with him in my life.

Tripp arrives in twenty-eight minutes, he felt it necessary to tell me that.

"One step closer to teleportation, dove."

Sitting back in his chair, he smiles over at me. "You do make a... *mean?* frittata."

I raise an eyebrow in triumph. "Told you."

"When did people start using the word mean as a positive adjective?"

Standing, I grab our plates, and he follows suit, clearing the rest of the table.

"No clue." I shrug, packing our plates into the dishwasher. "But it's all in the delivery."

He laughs, wiping down the table. His back is to me, and I watch the soft shake of his shoulders in affection. I like his laugh, more, I like *making* him laugh. It's a nice sound. One that warms parts of my body that I was certain had vacated the premises.

Turning, he catches my stare, his laugh trailing off, his gaze transforming in a blink, no longer amused, replaced with his lazy desire that pushes the rate of my pulse skyward.

Gait languorous, he stalks toward me. Footsteps slow to offer me the opportunity to reject his advance. The small of my back rested against the counter, I swallow down my nerves. It takes both forever and no time at all for him to reach me. In my peripheral I see his hands move, the hands I postulated to feel both calloused and tender. I was right, they're rough without being too callous, tender without being faint. Gripping my waist, he shifts our position, him now caged in against the counter.

The gesture tightens my throat at the thoughtfulness that lays inherently within him. It's unwavering.

"I'm gonna kiss you now, dove."

He leans forward.

"And I'm gonna kiss you back."

"See," he murmurs against the breath of space between my lips. "*Magic.*"

Tripp Tanner offers the ultimate in slow burn. His kisses start slow, a gentle caress of his lips against mine. He tastes, his tongue sweeping along my bottom lip in exploration.

Brady used to kiss me like I was his prey, devouring me with intense passion. Head tilted to the side he'd make certain he could taste every line of my mouth. He'd grab me roughly and kiss me the same way. His thirst was possession, power.

Tripp kisses me like I'm his queen, devouring me with deep worship. His craving is driven by *my* pleasure. Instead of belonging to a man, I feel part of him and he, part of me. Love is more powerful this way. Two wholes with the same feelings of devotion and worship. Wanting to give themselves over to the other. Not for completion, but for enrichment. A partner to weather the downs life weighs on your shoulders. A cheerleader to celebrate your wins.

Tentatively my tongue peeks out to touch his. He groans and I step into his body, enjoying the way the hard planes of his chest push against me. He licks into my mouth in lazy exploration. Unhurried, completely lost in a moment of *us*. Pausing every so often, his teeth graze my bottom lip, following the gentle bite with an even softer kiss. Tripp kisses in a way that hooks you from the second the heat of his breath skates along your lips. Intensity growing with every measured movement of his mouth. He knows how to kiss, and he knows how to kiss *well*. Every part of my body buzzes with the electricity sparked against my lips. I could kiss him forever and never want to come up for air.

My hands find the hem of his shirt, moving up to feel the burning heat of his skin. I whimper at the feel of him. Hard and hot, skin like silk and fire. Tripp groans, deepening our kiss, the sound humming against my lips forcing me to do the same.

He pulls away first. Our breaths heave between us, our chests pushing together, deflating apart only to touch again. Palm gripping his face, eyes wild with lust, he watches me.

"You're making me lose control, dove," he teases.

I don't tell him he does the same to me. He can read it well enough in the puffy pout of my well-kissed lips. In the liquid desire flowing through my wide eyes.

Stepping back, I reluctantly pull my hands from his shirt. I feel cold immediately, the torridity of his body no longer warming mine.

Standing to full height, he grips hold of the dishtowel. "You wash, I'll dry."

He shifts away from the sink and I move in, the sound of running water echoing between us, letting us run away with our thoughts.

"The birds on your arm, that tattoo." I turn to him, gesturing to the dark ink peeking from his shirt sleeve. "Do they symbolize anything?"

Glancing to his arm, he drops the dishtowel to the counter, pulling his sleeve up. My eyes are distracted by the corded muscle of his arm, the bulge in his bicep.

"They're actually bats," he clarifies. "Five of them."

Turning off the faucet, I step closer. "Huh. They are. I can't believe I didn't notice that before."

"The Chinese believe the bat represents both good fortune and longevity."

I listen to him talk with wonder. The sound of his voice soothing to the demons in my soul. Tripp Tanner is my balm, one I never want to give up.

"Five bats together," he continues, oblivious to my love-clouded brain. "Signifies more; the five blessings of a long life."

"Which are?" I reach out to touch each one, my fingertip gliding along his skin in affection.

"A long life."

He watches my touch, that wild lust firing up again, throat swallowing thickly.

"Wealth."

"Mm," I agree, my finger trailing up over his shoulder.

"Honor," he grits out, nostrils flaring in unhinged desire.

"Of course." I smile, fingertip dipping inside his shirt to run along his clavicle.

"Health." He swallows again, my eyes following them movement before my finger does, tracking over the thick bob of his Adam's apple.

"And finally." He steps closer, our bodies now flush, my arm caught between us, a breath from his lips. "A natural death."

Our eyes anchor and my ability to breathe abandons me.

"My mind is analytical," he explains. "But that's not how the world works. It took me some time to realize that; it's not all facts, figures, and clear answers. There's feeling and emotion that muddies waters. Your being, the person you are doesn't always abide by common sense, it's about what's in here." He points at his heart. "There's greater strength in the things we can't see."

"Are you even real?"

He answers me with a kiss, this time his hands fitting to my backside to pull me up. Legs wrapped around his waist, I kiss him back with fervor.

Ass placed on the counter, my hands cup his cheeks, fingers locked into his hair.

Pulling away from my mouth, his lips trail along my jaw.

This is a bad idea, my brain pushes into the haze of lust and I push it back away, hands dropping, pulling at his shirt.

Stepping back, he watches me for a beat, checking for any hesitation that may be swirling in my eyes. Confident in what he sees, his hand grips the back of his shirt at the neck, yanking it up and over his head.

Sweet mother of Jesus.

"Oh my God," I praise. "You're not real, are you?" I speak to his broad chest. "All this talk of magic, you're really Fae or something."

He laughs, loudly, neck tipped back, the sound rich and as potent as a drug, one I'd happily overdose on.

Righting his neck, he smiles at me. The open-mouthed smile, all his teeth on show, thick lines cut into his cheeks in happiness.

"It's true, Fae distract you with their exceptionally good looks." I gesture to the golden skin, liken to silk, covering the marble of his abdominal muscles. "I mean," I groan, the sound light and airy. "*No one* looks that good nearing forty."

"Thirty-six," he admonishes. "And *exceptionally* good looking, huh?"

I raise an eyebrow as he steps closer again. "Fishing for compliments, sir?"

"You betcha."

Now it's my turn to laugh, except this time he swallows it with a kiss. No precursor of soft nibbles or teasing tongues. Straight in; deep, hypnotic, and addictive.

This is dangerous, my mind warns me.

You're pushing yourself, it cautions.

Maybe it's true. Maybe I'm moving to a step I'm not one hundred percent ready for, but until I try, how do I know?

There's no rush, it tells me. *He doesn't need your body to fall in love with your heart.*

I hate my mind, the way it forces me to look into my greatest fears. How can I expect Tripp to stay, how can I ever expect his feelings to mirror mine when I'm keeping part of myself locked away from him?

I shush my doubts, weight them back down with the brush of my hands against his broad chest.

I can do this.

I *want* to do this.

"Couch," I mumble against his lips.

"You sure?" He pulls back. "We don't need to rush into anything, dove."

"*Please,*" I beg, severing his doubt with the sharp end of a blade.

Lifting me once again, he walks us through my apartment, lips sealed to mine the entire time.

The couch is soft against my back, his body hard against my front as he lays me down.

You're trapped.

I pull him closer, kissing him as deeply as I can.

Big hands find the hem of my shirt, peeling it up. I swallow my reservations.

Tripp. They're Tripp's hands, I tell myself.

Chest bare, he growls, one hand lifting my leg to wrap around his waist, the other cupping my breast, tongue dragging across my nipple.

My back arches and I moan. Euphoria courses through my body, breaking along my skin in goosebumps at the minor touch. Still, my body reacting positively doesn't ease the devil of my mind.

Don't move. He'll hurt you.

I roll my shoulders, elevating the tension coiling there without my permission.

"You good?" he checks on me, eyes darting to my lips and back again.

"Yeah," I lie, leaning up to claim his mouth, our tongues dancing. His hard and heavy with need, with desire; mine with the requisite of shutting out the thoughts stirring from the black hole swirling inside of me.

My body is shaking, and I can't be certain if it's from pleasure or fear. Same goes for my heart, currently racing in my chest, pounding with such ferocity it feels ready to burst from my body.

I draw in a deep breath through my nose, pushing it out of my lips with restraint as Tripp's tongue and mouth dance along my chest, down my sternum, back up and across to my bare nipples.

I'm sweating. My skin no longer comfortable, now flaming with the inferno of something I can't quite pinpoint, causing further scarring.

"*St-top,*" I whisper, the word catching in the dryness of

my throat, but he doesn't hear me, his lips moving upward kissing the column of my neck. Landing on my pulse point, he stops, tongue pressed against it to feel the unhealthy rhythm. His teeth graze the same spot and my body locks in place.

"Stop," I scream, the sound blood curdling raw.

Flying back as though I've burnt him, Tripp's chest heaves with panic.

"Dove." Hands held up in placation. "I'm so sorry. I got caught up. *Fuck,*" he spits.

Hands brushing over his face in a growl of attrition, I take the opportunity to crawl up the couch, cowering in the corner, cushion covering my naked body.

"Baby, shit, I'm *so* fucking sorry," he apologizes.

I shake my head, struggling to tell him he has nothing to be sorry for. This is me. Hopeless, broken me.

"I need you to leave," I whisper, a sob racking up my throat and forcing itself out in a hiccup.

"I don't really want to leave you alone, Taylor," he argues quietly. "Will you let me stay, I promise I won't touch you, I just want to make sure you're okay."

My head shakes in quick and jerky movements. "*Please.* I want to be alone."

He watches me for a beat, regret ashen on his face. He stands, defeat in his frame. I hear him wander into the kitchen, my body unable to unlock from the position I've forced myself into. Shirt back in place, he moves back toward me, crouching beside me, careful not to touch me.

"Me leaving right now is screaming against every integral facet of who I am. It doesn't feel right."

It's a plea, a hushed request to let him stay. One I can't grant him, so I remain silent.

"I rushed that, dove, and I can't apologize enough. I hope you can forgive me. Fuck, I hope you can do that. When you're up to it, *please* call me."

He waits for my confirmation, which I give through an erratic nod.

Kissing his fingertips, he presses them softly against my quivering lips.

"I'm sorry," I utter, the word like gravel against the rawness in my throat.

"You have *nothing* to be sorry for," he quarrels. "Look at me and promise you understand that."

Lifting my head, I feel my tears crawl from the corners of my eyes, dripping along the side of my face. "I understand that." My words are feeble and implausible, but on a deflated sigh, he accepts them, leaving my house feeling as broken as I do.

Five breaths. I count them. Stills of his tattooed bats like permanent marks in my mind. Five deep inhales of air into my lungs, released in the same way. Five breaths after my front door clicks closed for me to unravel completely. Thick, heavy sobs tormenting my body, making it shake with the power of my grief. And there I stay, late into the afternoon after the last of my tears have finally dried, body spent, my mind exhausted.

TWENTY

"Morning, sunshine."

"Hey," I mumble into the line, shifting out of the way of a suit storming down the sidewalk, paying no mind to anyone else.

"You sound like you didn't sleep at all last night."

Pausing to concentrate on her conversation, I plaster my back against the wall of the closest boutique along the path. "That's because I didn't."

"Has he called?"

Lifting my free hand, I place a finger against my ear, working to hear her better. "Last night, yeah, a few apology texts too. I can't believe *he's* apologizing to *me*. I was the one who acted the fool."

A scoff barks at me through the line. "First, you did not act like a fool, and since when did you start speaking like Mr. T?! Of course, he would apologize. Not saying he was in the wrong," she argues. "But his actions forced your mind into a place it didn't want to go."

I sigh. "Maybe."

"Not maybe," she gripes. "Have you called him back?"

I swallow. "Yeah, just before you called, but it went to voicemail."

"What about Hannah?" she asks.

I glance around the streets, watching the few people out rush about their day. I don't even know where I am, or what I'm doing. I left home needing air, without a purpose. I'm wandering, which is so unlike me, yet, here I am. Standing on a random Manhattan street watching one man clean up after his dog who decided to relieve his bowels on the sidewalk, and another check his watch consistently, glancing up and down the relatively deserted street for a cab.

"I tried her a few times last night," I offer absently. "But she wasn't online, and she's not responding to my texts."

"That sucks. Does that happen often?"

"No," I frown. "Not really, but she was acting off last time I spoke to her as well. Probably another patient," I surmise.

A cab blares its horn for no apparent reason causing me to grimace.

"Where *are* you?"

I shrug before realizing she can't see me. "I don't know. I needed out of the house. I went for a walk. Now I'm standing on some street watching some dude pick up dog crap."

"Gross."

"Hmm," I agree, turning away to look down the street, working to find my bearings. "There's a coffee shop, I might go there and grab an iced coffee."

"Want me to meet you?"

I consider her offer. "At home? I might just get it to go. Want something?"

"Yeah, a latte." I hear her front door close. "Catch you in fifteen or so?"

"Yep. Bye." I hang up, stuffing my cell into my pocket.

Throughout my life I've had people tell stories of how they met their best friend, how they just *clicked*. I thought it a falsehood. A made up story by people who had known each other forever. I've had friends in my life, sure. Close ones, ones at the time I'd deem as my best.

But I've never had a Rae.

I get it now. From the moment she sat beside me at book club... there was an innate connection. A foundation that had established by the time she'd introduced herself. It's odd in the same way it's freeing. *I* have a person. A friend I can tell *any*thing to and she listens. Not only is she not afraid to call me on my shit. She's considerate of my feelings but not to a point that it's detrimental to me in any way. She doesn't enable, more, she challenges me to be the person I *want* to be.

I have someone in my life, for the first time in as long as I remember, that I trust implicitly. I don't have to pretend with Rae. She sees me. The real me. The broken down girl fighting to get back up, and without agenda, she's there helping me stand.

Like now, she knows emotionally and most likely, mentally, I'm in a vulnerable state. Without me needing to vocalize it, she knows I need her, and more, she doesn't hesitate to *be* there.

A sense of calm settles through my bones at the thought. Rae accepts me for who I am, and if that isn't the defining pinnacle of friendships, I don't know what is.

Taking a step in the direction of the coffee shop, I shiver. It's cold. Icy wind ripping between the buildings and slicing against my skin like the lash of a whip. I'm annoyed at myself for stupidly leaving my apartment without a jacket or a beanie. I was in such a rush to escape my own thoughts, I didn't second guess what I was doing.

Arms wrapped around my body, I shuffle my feet along quicker, considering I might give the iced coffee a miss, hot coffee might be better placed. My hands ache at the thought of holding something warm and I absently clench my fists against my arms, rubbing them along the thin line of my shirt.

Ducking my head against the wind, I move with purpose, destination... *coffee.*

I try not to think about the fact that Tripp hasn't called me back. My anxiety taking hold and running riot in my mind. He's finally seen I'm not worth the trouble. I don't even blame him for giving up. It hurts, more than I imagined it would. A hole is burning deep in my gut, growing bigger with every unanswered second that passes.

Not knowing if he's *with* me feels like I'm missing part of myself. The part he'd spent the last few months helping me reclaim. He gave it to me and I never imagined how easy it would be for him to take it back. Only this time I feel emptier, the void more poignant, more pronounced.

Lifting my head as I near the coffee shop, I all but trip over my own feet. It's like I'd conjured him into life. Thick wide strides crossing the street with purpose, his eyes darting to his cell, clasped desperately in his hand, before reading the sign with a determination that is so perfectly him my heart aches.

It's the first time I've seen him look anything but poised. Hair disheveled, clothes haphazardly thrown on, he looks as well as I feel. Trodden down. His challenging and confident nature giving place to a look of uncertainty, generally more at home on me. Like me, he looks like he hasn't slept, the sockets under his eyes sunken and bruised.

He doesn't see me, too consumed with his objective to consider the world around him. But this I already know about him.

I could call out. Speak his name loud enough to be heard over the non-existent sound of the street. Unsurprisingly I don't. In truth, I'm hurt. He's not away from his phone. Instead, the small device was held protectively in his hand. Which means even if he didn't see my call come through, he's most definitely made the decision *not* to call me back.

Ouch.

Yanking the door open harder than necessary, he storms through, disappearing from sight. My feet shuffle backward, readying to flee, but something within me freezes them in place. I'm stuck.

I could walk away. *Run.* Abscond my problems, hide from my life as soon as an upward spike places itself in my path. Like always.

Or... I could find my backbone and walk through the door of the coffee shop and *talk* to him.

He's important to me. He says I'm important to him and I'm not quite sure I can walk away without some form of closure. If Tripp has made the decision that my broken soul is too much work, I should at least know. Right? I won't pine. I won't worry. I'll know exactly where I stand.

I roll my eyes at myself. Yeah, Zoe, because it's *that* easy.

God, it's moments like this I wish Rae were here.

She'd push me forward.

She'd tell me to stop being afraid. That it was as easy as placing one foot in front of the other.

And she'd be right.

If I had my jacket, I'd have my chess piece. I'd have my *queen*. I'd have the small wooden symbol of my strength to push me forward. But I don't, so I have to find it in myself.

Leaving Brady was hard, telling him I was done, that I couldn't do *us* anymore a memory I likely won't ever forget. He fought me on it of course, but by that stage I was so devoid of human emotion that I just stared at him. Seemingly *un*feeling. He hated that. My detachment.

This though, my heart has opened like the delicate petals of a spring bloom. I've become vulnerable to love, which means I've also exposed myself to the possibility of heartbreak. Talk about a double-edged sword. Making you weak just before cutting you down.

Closing my eyes, I inhale deeply through my nose. The cold air burns my nostrils, stinging my sinus. I let the bite of my breath creep to the very top of my head, holding it there for a single beat before letting it seep out of me. I exhale with purpose, like Hannah and meditation and mindfulness has taught me. Expelling the negative energy; my nerves, my anxiety, my indecision, from my body in bursts. My face, my shoulders, my diaphragm, and tummy all softening as I dictate.

Because *I'm* in control.

The queen in my own story.

Letting my eyes fall open, I roll my fingers into my palm, clenching my fists before releasing.

One foot in front of the other.

I make it to the door of the coffee shop without fanfare, without issue, and I almost pat myself on the back in pride.

That all dissolves into nothing as my hand reaches for the door.

I'm swallowed up by a dark hole of numb. A gray cloud surrounding me, threatening to pull out of this new life I'm building, to place me directly back into the past, I'd up until now, been content in settling within.

I blink, once, twice, shaking my head to refocus. I *have* to be seeing things. It's the only explanation as to why, in this random coffee shop, in the middle of Manhattan, Tripp Tanner, my *boyfriend,* is sitting across from my therapist lost in conversation like they're old friends.

Hannah looks poised as always, only this time a pinch of something I can't quite determine is twisting her usual serene features. Their bodies allude connection, leaned in toward one another like they're well acquainted... I feel torn, caught between my need to know more and my desire to run away. To remain in my oblivion about their relationship.

You couldn't write it if you tried. Me stumbling across this very scene. What are the odds? You see it in movies. You read it in books. The ill-timed crossing of paths unraveling a secret people had so artfully crafted, certain they'd never be found out.

I watch their interaction with intrigue. It's not kind. In fact, animosity swirls chaotically between them. Leaning across the table, Tripp listens to Hannah speak, his head shaking. Maybe in dismissal, possibly disbelief. It's too hard to tell not hearing what they're actually saying. Hannah points a finger in accusation, and I watch Tripp's face drop.

My cell rings, and I absently pull it from my pocket.

"Yo." Rae speaks into the line. "You there?"

"Yeah," I mumble.

"What's up?" The quiet hesitance in her tone forces my feet away from the door, across the façade of the shop.

"Tripp is here," I tell her, peering into the window. "With Hannah."

A pause. "I didn't realize they knew one another."

I swallow the lump of tension in my throat. "Me either."

"*Ohhh*," she drawls. "Have you approached them?"

I scowl at my reflection in the glass. "Of course not."

"Well, go up to them. Figure out what the fuck is going on."

"No."

"No?" she balks. "Zoe. They're both keeping something from you—"

"I've gotta go," I cut her off, ending the call without waiting for her to respond.

It's always shocked me how great the effect your emotions inflict on your body. I'm shaking. Unintentionally. My insides are quaking, forcing my heart to flutter noticeably in my chest. I can't even adequately determine the emotion wreaking such havoc.

Am I mad?

I don't think so. I've felt rage before, and it didn't feel *anything* like this.

Am I sad?

Again, I can't say that I am. How can I be when I'm not actually sure as to *what* I'm seeing?

I think mostly I'm surprised, definitely uncertain. Anxious, yes. Disappointed, definitely.

My skin feels clammy, which is ridiculous considering

how cool the air around me is. I went from shivering against the cold to sweating with the fire of shock licking my skin.

Without warning, Tripp stands, color fading from his face, eyes wide with uncertainty as he turns his back on Hannah, rushing from the shop. I turn and duck my head, hiding in plain sight. But he doesn't notice. Too caught up in his own thoughts to offer anyone else consideration. I watch his retreat down the sidewalk, his feet moving him the direction I only minutes ago came from. Shoulders sagging in defeat, he hunches against the cold.

Only when he's out of sight do I turn back to Hannah, still settled in her seat; blank and unmoving.

My cell sounds in my pocket, but I pay it no mind, my focus on the woman I'd relied so heavily on for too many years. The woman who I shared the deepest, darkest, most damaged parts of myself with. The woman I counted as a friend.

She barely raises her head as I slide into the seat, still warmed from Tripp's presence. Her eyes are glassed over, tears brimming along the bottom line of her lashes, readying themselves to spill onto her face.

"Did you set it up?" I ask quietly. "Tripp and me," I clarify. "A push to move me out of my comfort zone, into the land of the living. Was it a test?"

Lifting her face, her eyes clashing against mine, the tears no longer threatening to spill, now an obvious stream of regret gliding across her cheeks.

She shakes her head, an almost imperceptible move, but I see it, the quick side-to-side of her head. "No."

I believe her. I don't know why. I guess seeing her looking as broken as I feel inside gives reason to the fact that she no longer has anything to hide. I saw her. I saw *them*. What would be the point?

"Do you know him?"

"No," she answers with more confidence in her voice, a hand rising to wipe away her tears. "I don't."

I wait quietly, giving her the opportunity to offer me the truth. Explain what the hell is happening.

"I can't be your therapist anymore." She stuns me by declaring.

My thoughts are obviously painted openly on my face because she takes a breath to speak.

Tongue caught between her lips, her eyes focus on the table separating us. It's the first time in the copious hours we've spent talking that I've seen her unsure.

"I stepped over the line," she explains. "I've *been* stepping over the line. I've stopped seeing you as a client," she admits shamefully. "I see you as a friend. I've become too close, Zoe."

I shrug, unconcerned by her confession. "We are friends."

"That's an issue, Zoe. It's a conflict, I can't adequately treat you, I can no longer remain objective. I have a set bias to your happiness as your friend. That inhibits me from being able to offer appropriate advice. I'm too invested," she offers quietly.

She's torn up by her own declaration. Failure sits heavily in her eyes, pleading with me for forgiveness.

"That doesn't explain...."

Hands to her forehead, she pauses, bringing her hands to her mouth in a prayer-like gesture. Moving to rest her clasped hands under her chin, she clears her throat.

"You said his name, his *full* name for the first time in our last session."

"Tripp Tanner?" I question.

"The name, it tickled my curiosity. A lawyer with the surname *Tanner.*"

I frown. "I don't understand."

"Miller Jacobs' lawyer," she whispers.

My heart stutters at his name, my frown deepening. "I... He..."

"Theo Tanner," she speaks just as quietly as before.

I remember the man like I'd crossed paths with him only yesterday.

A statuesque man, age lines prominent on his face, hair graying. A confidence not out of place in a courtroom; he played dirty. He humiliated me. He pulled apart every last detail of my life. My family. My friendships. My relationship. My *sex* life. He paraded Miller as a victim. *My* victim. A woman not satisfied in her relationship, I'd clearly dabbled elsewhere, regretting my actions when Brady discovered my indiscretion.

I was the only person at fault by his account. A falsehood he painted with limited flaw. He cornered me. Dangled a plea for Miller in front of my lawyer, which she convinced me to agree to.

It was a fifty-fifty shot, she said.

We could win, *maybe* just *maybe* the bite mark and GHB in my system were enough for a rape conviction to stick.

We could also lose. Miller Jacobs could walk from that courtroom without a blemish to his name. Theo Tanner was *that* convincing.

Indecent assault. That was the charge in the end. The plea that Miller's lawyer had convinced him to cop to. Not rape. An aggravated assault of a sexual nature.

I googled the hell out of rape statistics when my lawyer approached me with the charge. Less than one percent of rape cases end in convictions. Less than *one* percent. No wonder the crime is so devastatingly unreported. Why bother? Your assailant will likely walk, why put yourself through the trauma.

"He's Tripp's dad, Zoe."

I close my eyes, refusing to hear her. The faint drum of her voice hitting inside like a bullet directly at my heart.

My head shakes, my chin involuntarily wobbling in denial. "No."

"I just couldn't shake the name. I googled him. He's set to take over his father's firm."

Tripp told me that himself.

"I remember reading through the news coverage over your trial that Miller had a close familial connection with the lawyer."

"Don't say his name." I can't even conjure a coherent thought. Elbows to the table, I rip at my hair, trying to calm the storm of my mind.

"You're lying," I accuse, my head refusing to stop shaking, denying her claim.

"Zoe," she implores.

"Why would you make up such a horrible thing? What? You're alluding to the fact that Tripp knows who I am? That *they* planned this."

"No," she denies, caught off-guard by my accusation.

"Why are you doing this? You just expect me to believe that Tripp, my *boyfriend,* the man I've fallen in *love* with," I confess surprisingly, both electrified and unsettled at the ease in which I can admit that. "The man who has brought me back to life," I sob. Humiliatingly I *sob*. Unable to stop the monsoon of emotion from breaking free. "You're telling me" — I take a breath, steeling my composure— "that it was all fake. That what I felt can't be real because he's not real."

I'm aware of the bite in my words. The uncharacteristic fire igniting my voice to ensure everyone within the coffee shop is brought into my story.

She leans closer. "I'm not doing this to hurt you," she panics. "I didn't believe it at first myself."

"So what," I yell, the soft chatter in the space surrounding us dying off as eyes settle on us. "You just happened to *stumble* across the connection? I should just believe that?"

I want to break something. How dare she do this. How dare she unravel my life so severely without consulting me first.

"You're mad," she whispers. "And you have every right to be. I should've come to you first. Let you discuss this with Tripp."

I scowl at her. "You absolutely should've come to me fucking first. Why didn't you? Why call him? That's what you did, right?" I spit. "You called him, asked him to meet you."

She nods.

"Why? Why would you do that? I pay you, remember? What the hell do you owe him?"

"This is what I'm saying," she cries. "I'm too invested. I needed to know his game before dropping this on you."

"Oh." I laugh humorlessly. "Now you're my savior."

My anger is ill-directed. I don't know what to feel, what to think. My world, the one I've spent the past few months building into something I crave, something I thought I was afraid of, is crashing down at lightning speed, and once again I find myself powerless.

"*Zoe*," Hannah appeases.

"You're wrong," I state confidently. "You have to be. I'm gonna call Tripp, he'll explain. He'll tell us you've confused him with someone else." I'm pleading with her, my eyes boring into hers, begging her to take it back.

I *need* her to take it back.

I *need* her to be wrong.

"You're mistaken," I repeat, the fight in my voice gone.

"Breathe," she mollifies.

I follow her lead, doing as she instructs.

"He was just as shocked as we were," she divulges. "He didn't know, Zoe."

I don't speak, even if I found the ability to do so, words are forgotten. What is there to be said anyway?

My fingers rub together, memorizing the queen that I could really use right now.

I imagine it in my hand, the carved wooden piece, worn down over the years, but still a shield I'm not ready to leave behind.

"I accused him of knowing," Hannah explains. "He was so confused. Every time I said your name, your *real* name, he looked at me like I was speaking a foreign language. He thought I'd confused him with someone else. I had to explain that you were Zoe, that Taylor Smith *was* Zoe Lincoln."

"*How?*"

She knows me well enough to know what I'm asking. "It's one hell of a coincidence."

I swallow. "Is it though? *Really?*"

"What does he have to gain from manipulating you into a relationship?"

I think of the pain that Miller Jacobs inflicted in my life. "To break me. Finally."

Sadness closes her eyes. "I believe him," she admits. "He looked ripped in two when he pieced it all together."

That sounds nice, preferable to how I feel, shredded into a million and one pieces. Fragments lost on the floor, discarded with no hope of ever being glued back together.

"Coffee?" Hannah offers.

I nod.

Grabbing my hand, she squeezes. "It's just another road-block. I know it seems hopeless, but you'll work it out. I promise."

I stare at her for a beat. "Yeah."

She doesn't believe my lackluster response. Not that I blame her, I have no belief in it myself. Still, she turns, moving toward the counter to order.

Her back facing me, I take my opportunity, standing, I move from the coffee shop, ignoring the eyes watching my escape.

TWENTY-ONE

The cool air feels like a sucker punch to the chest, robbing me of air.

I gulp. My failed inhale twisted harshly with the sob I let go. It hurts. The sound. Listening to your heart split roughly down the middle. Louder than any bomb blast, any gunshot. The deafening tear so viciously raw it feels as though a hand has pushed through your chest bone. Bones shattered as the very organ keeping you alive is pulled from your body without regard.

I felt empty after Miller. Numb. Like I'd died. Which is what I thought I wanted for a time. This though, this is different. I'd give my life to be suffocated by that numb once again. This time, I feel *everything*.

Overwhelmed by every negative feeling you could possibly conjure, my body is trembling, *quaking*, readying itself to explode into a million irredeemable pieces.

I begin walking, my feet rushing home with the need to hide away.

Safe.

My bubble.

My sanctuary.

I ignore the incessant ring of my phone buzzing continuously in my pocket. People look at me rush past with a mixture of concern and condemnation lining their faces. I look a mess. I have no doubt. Eyes red-rimmed, skin blotchy, hair blowing around my face like a whip. I don't attempt to tame it, letting it inhibit my ability to see. I'm shaking. From both the cold and my overwrought anxiety.

I'm mad. So *fucking* mad. Irate. I'd finally started to piece my life back together. I'd slowly began building the life that *I* wanted. That I deserved. I'd activated the warrior everyone had spent years convincing me was living inside of me. I'd battled against every war Miller and my own demonic mind had forced me to endure. I was winning, goddammit.

I was winning.

It has taken me so long to find the realization that my happiness is important... To get to a point where I can look at my reflection in the mirror and feel deserving.

Tripp, Rae, Rake, they pushed me, they ignited the fire within me, and I chose to live. After so long of contentedly wasting away, they showed me the *more* of life.

Now I'm staring down the barrel of my own demise once again.

Defeat. Surrender.

I've come full circle. It's what the universe wants. I'm certain of it. My surrender. My self-proclaimed defeat.

But why?

What the hell did I ever do to anyone?

Was it a past life indiscretion that was so bad, karma had to make sure it kicked me in the ass in this life too?

Maybe that's how it works. Karma. Maybe you pay for your sins in the following life, just to ensure moving into the one after you don't continue down your paved path to hell.

Maybe that's when Miller will finally pay his penance. He escaped his sins of today with little ramification. Stepping into a life of tomorrow, maybe hell will hath no fury.

It's an evil cycle I've let my mind wander to. If it's true, and I'm paying for the sins of a Zoe from before, does that make my hell justified?

It's impossible. I've spent years in therapy clawing my way out of self-blame, and in the flick of time, it can all come crashing down.

The warmth of my apartment building hits me poetically as I step through the lobby door. A warmth wrapping around me like a winter fire, impossibly working to quell the ice inside my heart.

My feet trudge up the stairs, stumbling as my apartment comes into view.

Sitting against my door is Rae, legs crossed at the ankles, worry furrowing her brow as Tripp paces in front of her. They're silent, save Tripp's footsteps.

"Zoe." Rae stands, glancing to Tripp cautiously and rushing forward.

I let her hug me, but fail to reciprocate the gesture. My eyes remain trained on a now still Tripp. He looks as lost as I do.

His eyes scan me as though he's seeing me for the very first time. Like I'm a stranger that offers him a sense of deja vu. Familiar, but also so significantly foreign to his conscience.

Handing my key to Rae without a word, she takes it,

opening my door without speaking. I follow her into my apartment, pausing on the threshold.

"Did you know?"

Tripp steps forward, forcing me backward, entering my apartment and closing us into the space that was once my haven.

"Hannah says you didn't," I pause, swallowing the break in my voice. "But I need you to tell me you didn't know. *Please* tell me you had no idea who I was."

"I didn't know," he declares as quietly as he does vehemently.

Without looking, I know Rae has made herself scarce, the room filled solely with mine and Tripp's presence, suffocating us both in despair.

"How did this happen?" I challenge, not specifically to him, but to the room. To the clouds of circumstance whirling around us like a tornado.

Hands tucked into his pockets, he shrugs.

"How do you know him?" I hate myself for even asking, for the tragic curiosity rising in my voice.

"He's my best friend." His face breaks; eyes closing tightly, head shaking, jaw wiring shut. "I've known him my whole life."

He would've been better to take his fist and lodge it powerfully into my gut. I stumble backward, hands lifting to stabilize my emotion.

My hands tremble, a soft stutter sounding from my lips bracketing my heartbreak.

"Did you know?" I accuse. "What he did to me... Did you know?"

Pulling his hands from his pockets, his palms find the back of his head, elbows touching to hide his face.

My mind, my soul, my *heart* is begging him to say no. To deny *any* knowledge of the monster that is his *best friend*.

Elbows spreading apart, his eyes stare at me in pain.

"Tell me," I demand.

"I believed you lied."

"What?" I breathe.

He looks rightfully ashamed, but it doesn't take away from the confidence in his declaration. The belief in the words he just sliced me open with.

"I've known him all my life, Zoe." He uses my real name, bringing the gravity of the moment to the forefront. The ghost I'd put to sleep stirring with grandeur. "What he was accused of... He told me he didn't do it and I believed him."

I feel as though I've been stripped naked, bare, my scars laid open like the most unholy of sacrifices.

"I had a boyfriend at the time," I start. "But you know that."

He nods.

"I was happy." My face shows no recollection of the afore-mentioned emotion, instead, my face is bleeding with pain. *"We* were happy, me and Brady, contrary to the picture your father painted. So when Miller approached me in that bar, I chose not to engage. That, and the guy gave me a creepy vibe. My instincts were right."

Tripp scratches his neck uncomfortably. "You don't have to tell—"

"Oh, but I do," I cut him off angrily. "You heard his side of the story, you can hear mine. You can hear how *pissed off* he was at my rejection," I grit out.

A chill, colder than ice grips the very base of my spine holding my ability to stand at ransom. One quick flick and the strength in my backbone is broken. Cracked beyond repair. Just like my heart, like my spirit. What's the ability to stand when the rest of you is just as broken.

"He apologized at the end of the night, or what I *thought* was the end of his night," I correct myself.

Hand lifting, my fingers rub along my lips, tasting that last soda like it had just wet my lips. "I was drinking soda; he lied about that too. I wasn't drunk. I wasn't high. Like I told you, I've never been a drinker. I was sober before he drugged me."

"Zoe," he appeals. For what I'm not quite sure.

"A lot of the night is hazy, but I remember the worst parts." I'm crying, I hadn't even realized I'd started, but as salt dries my skin and my nose runs like a tap, my words stutter along my jagged breaths. But I continue. "I remember feeling completely powerless." I close my eyes. "Weak, feeble, *pathetic.*"

I'm not a pretty crier. My nose itches and I rub it, wiping my snot on the sleeve of my shirt to stop it running. Saliva builds in my mouth in panic, my eyes stinging with the razor sharpness of my tears, making them swell on my face. Through it all, Tripp watches on in pity. *Pity.*

"I felt so horribly alone," I tell him, working to ignore the weakness he sees so evidently in me. "There were people *every*where to begin with, but none of them would *help* me," I plead with him to understand the desperation I had felt. "Powerless and alone," I muse. "I can't imagine a more despondent way to feel."

I clear my throat, and still he heeds, watching, listening, hearing my story.

"He pushed me on his bed—"

"Stop," he cuts me off, but I shake my head, a smile so tainted with hate crawling onto my face.

"And all of a sudden I was *naked*. I can't recall him taking my clothes off... your dad used that against me in court. He said I took them off, that consent was skewed because me removing my clothing indicated to your friend that I was into it. I didn't take my own clothes off, Tripp," I tell him, afraid he won't believe me. "I know that because I never planned to be there in the first place."

He says nothing. He gives me no indication as to whether Miller's lie continues to be his truth, or whether he believes me. It infuriates me that he's put me in a position where I feel the need to defend myself.

"I struggled for a bit," I endure, pushing my self-worth to the side, my memories as agonizing as that very night, forcing me to relive every desperate second. "I said no. I did," I beseech. "His response was to..." I lift my hand, wrapping it around my neck in demonstration. "Wrap his hand around my neck so tight I couldn't breathe."

He swallows his own bile, the acid twisting his face in distaste.

As my story unfolds, I find my voice rising, spiked with fury, my anger directing itself at Tripp. At the man I'd slowly been opening my heart to, who believed me to be a liar.

"He'd whisper things in my ear like, '*I could kill you, so easily. Come on, Zoe, maybe you'll enjoy it.*'"

I watch his fists clench and release.

Clench. Release.

"I didn't," I confess unsurprisingly. "Enjoy it. He made sure of that. There was one moment that I found my full voice throughout the whole ordeal... I *screamed*, I begged for someone to help me."

My leg throbs in pain, the agony of his bite so real I could've sworn he'd only just done it, blood trickling down my skin from the ferocity in his jaw.

"He bit me," I spit, lifting the leg of my shorts, forcing him to see that scar Miller has tattooed permanently into my skin. "So *fucking* hard I still have the scar. Does that look like a lie to you?"

Tripp takes a step forward, his need to protect, to *ease* written all over his face.

I step backward, refusing him the task he so desperately seeks.

"The *pain* his teeth imprinted on me is like nothing I've ever felt. But even the brutal tear of my skin was nothing compared to the agony he tore my soul apart with."

I've fed him my pain. Forced it down his throat. Twisted my knife of agony into his heart and left it there to bleed. A tear falls from his eye and I watch its journey across his skin, down the valley of his cheek, along the line of his jaw.

"That's why you do what you do, isn't it?" I indict softly. "The pro bono work."

His palm coming up, he rubs the salty dampness from his skin. "Yes." His voice cracks, so he repeats it. "Yes."

We've just had the bomb of all realization dropped on us. We're standing on the ruins of what could've been, mere steps apart, but the weight of the world separating us.

I feel broken. I feel lost.

Tripp looks as destroyed as I am, yet, I don't have it in me to care. I'm so caught up in my own misery, his only enrages me further.

"I want you to leave."

His eyebrows pull together. "What? No. We need to talk."

"I said leave," I scream, panic clawing up my throat.

He takes a step backward. "I haven't done anything wrong," he refutes. "I'm just as caught off guard as you are."

"You called me a liar," I spit.

He shakes his head, turning to walk to the door. "No, I didn't. I said I believed you *had* lied. But that was before I knew it was you. That was when my trust had been ill placed in the hands of someone I believed to be *good."*

Hand on the door handle he pauses once again. "Reason I asked you to stop was because I didn't need your story to know you were telling the truth, dove. As soon as Hannah told me who you were, I knew I'd been the worst kind of fool. My loyalty skewed my ability to see clearly. I may be an idiot, but I'm innocent in this fucking mess. Just like you."

I watch him walk through the door, dragging my tattered heart along with him.

"You okay?"

I glance at Rae, looking away before she can read the heartbreak in my eyes. "Peachy."

"Zoe." I hear her move toward me, but I whirl on her, holding my hands up to stop her approach.

"I'd like you to leave."

Her face twists as though I've slapped her. "Not gonna happen."

My throat constricts, my eyes sting with the tears that I no longer have. "Just leave," I yell, needing to be left alone to break without an audience.

Rae's arms cross against her chest.

"You've clearly not had too many friends that stick by you the way they should've. You're working to push me away before I can abandon you."

My nostrils flare in panic.

"Your friends sucked," she bites out. "I, however, do not. You can flip out, you can yell, you can fucking scream, shit, you can be as nasty as you fucking want. Here's something you need to get through that pretty little head of yours... I'm not going anywhere."

I blink.

"You're stuck with me, because we're *friends*. And right now, what you need is a fucking friend. Break, Zoe, that's what I'm fucking here for, to be your shoulder to lean on, to pick you back up when you've fallen."

My knees give out, but she catches me before the ground does. Thick, ugly sobs break against her shoulder, one barely finished before the next takes its place. The sound echoes through my apartment, cutting through me like a serrated knife, making me cry harder. All the while her arms remain wrapped around me, holding me up.

Just like she promised.

TWENTY-TWO

TRIPP

My head is swimming. A violent storm of thoughts and emotions clashing together like waves along the shoreline. Destined to break, to fall apart into nothing but whitewash, into *nothing*. I can't even begin to coherently bring the pieces of this fucked up jigsaw together.

None of them fit. All open-ended pieces with nothing to interlock. Because none of it makes sense. How could it? *Fucking how?*

Rubbing at my eyes, I walk along *Zoe's* street. Zoe. Zoe Lincoln. The woman I'd scorned many a time for falsely accusing my best friend of sexual assault. Of *rape*.

I'd believed him. Without a doubt. Of course I did, I've known him my *entire* life, I *knew* him, the person he was inside. Or so I thought.

Her story changed, he assured me.

The evidence was weak at best, my dad guaranteed.

That's why they told me to stay in the UK. A stupid girl who cheated on her boyfriend and screamed rape to save face.

Jesus fucking Christ. How did I believe that?

I wanted to. Fuck did I want to. What was the alternative? To explore the possibility that my best friend was a sexual *predator*.

No way. Not Miller.

But it's true. I know that now. A man I'd put my trust in, one I'd welcomed into my family was nothing more than a monster that preyed on women.

You can't fake the life Zoe is living. It's not possible. From the moment I laid eyes on her right up until the moment I left her apartment, both metaphorically and literally closing the door on our relationship, there's no falsehood to her. Everything she speaks, verbal or otherwise, is truth. That's where she hides, in plain sight.

My mind plays her story on a reoccurring loop. The pain in her eyes forever engrained into my brain like a tattoo. Lies can be spoken, they can be spilled from your lips and swallowed without hesitation. But your truth sits within the crevices of your soul, shining out of your eyes, *waiting* to be seen.

Zoe's truth is bleeding from her eyes. You don't even have to look hard to see it. I knew from the second I saw her she'd been through a hell not many of us would ever have to endure. I didn't doubt her story when she confided in me about the stranger in the bar. Which means, the second Hannah Backhaus called me and told me the truth, I knew Miller had lied.

My best friend is a rapist, what's more, my dad protected him knowing what he'd done.

Feet stopping, I flag down the first cab I see. I bite out the address to my dad's office, an emotion far more potent than anger bubbling under my skin.

"Mr. Tanner." My dad's receptionist smiles at me warmly. "We weren't expecting you."

"Have someone bring me all records surrounding the Lincoln v. Jacobs case," I greet her insensitively. "I'll be in my office. Be quick."

Her eyes widen at the animosity in my tone, completely out of character and ill-directed. "Of course."

I nod, turning on my heel to stalk toward my office.

Hours later, boxes emptied across every available space of my office, I sit amongst the wrongs of my father. Ass to the floor, I slump against the wall, head tipped back.

"Rachel called," my dad speaks, forcing my eyes to open.

Standing against the framework of my office door, he's the picture of serenity.

"Said you were acting *odd*. Want to tell me what you're doing with Miller's case files?"

Dropping the paper in my hands to the ground, watching it land on another scrap of evidence that proves Miller's guilt, I rub at my jaw.

"Her story didn't change," I muse, throat dry from under-use, the words rough enough to make me clear my throat. "Not once. Not from the moment she reported the incident."

Stepping into my office, he steps over the evidence of his lies, settling into the first available armchair.

"What do you care?"

"The bite mark on her leg was so barbaric it's still there... did you know that? Tattooed into her skin like a birthmark she never wanted."

He has the decency to look ashamed. "How would you know that?"

I laugh sardonically. "I met her in New York. Of course

she goes by a different name now so I had no idea who she was... I fell in love with her. What are the fucking odds of that? I fell in love with the woman my best friend drugged, assaulted, and raped."

My father's eyes close and it's the first time I notice how tired he is, how much he's aged over the years. Guilt will do that to you though, eat away at your will to live.

"Did he tell you or did you just know?"

Refusing me eye contact, his gaze skates across the floor. "He told me. I thought I was doing the right thing, son. He's *family*."

"He's a rapist," I spit, pushing myself up, body towering with the anger bristling within me. "He's a fucking rapist. How *could* you?"

He says nothing, but then what *could* he say. There's no excuse, no reasoning what he did.

"He drugged this girl because she rejected him," I grit out. "Everyone that should've helped her abandoned her. The security guard, the cab driver, the hotel staff, her fucking friends. He made certain she was disoriented enough to be compliant, but awake enough to feel it."

He swallows his regret, face twisting as the acid of his decision burns his esophagus.

"When she tried to fight back, he strangled her." I pick up the photos from her hospital visit, the purple bruises along her neck, perfect fingerprints pressed into her skin. I throw them at him, watching his eyes close again as they fall around him. "He bit her," I bellow, frisbeeing the photos of that soul-wrenching image at his face, watching it bounce off his forehead to the floor.

"Then," I yell, "he took his fucking cock and *forced* it into her body. And you *defended* him. Worse, you convinced her fucking lawyer to make her take a deal."

"Tripp," he placates.

"How?" I ask. "How did you convince the lawyer?"

He shrugs. "She was relatively new. Rape cases are almost impossible to win. She knew that. I knew that. A lot of the evidence was circumstantial."

I see red. "*Circumstantial?*"

"Tripp." He stands, eyes pleading.

"I never want to see your face ever again. You're dead to me." I grab my jacket, pausing at the door. "As far as I'm concerned, I have no fucking father. Miller is your *family*, live happily with that."

I texted Miller as soon as I left my dad's office. Told him I was going to be in town and drove five hours non-stop to Charlottesville. But sitting in the car now, my heart thumps with indecision. I could drive away and be done with this scumbag for the rest of my life. But that almost seems too easy. Sentenced to six years, he served three. *Three fucking years.* Not a day more. After what he did, he deserves to rot for the rest of his days. Vindictive motherfucker.

Rolling my shoulders, I force myself to take five deep

breaths, calming the storm of anxiety within my chest. The climb from my car is fired and angry, door slammed, feet moving in quick strides toward the bar Miller requested I meet him, giving thought to the fact that my attempt at calm was a waste of twenty seconds.

The bar is dimly lit, relatively crowded and I pause at the door, scanning the premises. Stopping on him almost immediately, a scowl forms on my face automatically. Talking to a woman, he doesn't notice me, and I watch him as closely as I can from this distance.

Will he drug her?

How many times has he done it before?

Will he do it again, even after serving time?

Striding toward him, his smile grows as he sees me, a touch to the woman's shoulder to excuse himself as he steps around her to meet me.

Two steps from him, my fist rises on its own accord, smacking into his nose on a satisfying crunch. Bloods spurts from his nose like a waterfall, spilling over the bottom of his face and his shirt.

"The fuck?" he mumbles behind his hand, cupping his broken nose.

Not satisfied, I rear my fist back again, this time connecting it against his upper torso.

A pained grunt bends him in half, and I take the opportunity, palm to the crown of his head I push him with all my might watching as he falls to the floor.

Hand brushing through my hair, I stand over him, chest heaving in the need to continue my attack.

The crowd around us has dissipated, still present, drinks

in hand, watching the show like a staged production they'd paid to see.

"What the fuck is wrong with you?" He spits blood on the floor, rubbing his mouth with the back of his hand.

"What's wrong with me?" I yell. "Zoe Lincoln, remember her? *That's* what's wrong with me, you lying sack of shit."

Eyebrows to his hairline he shakes his head. "Don't know what you're talking about."

Crouching down, I look him directly in his evil fucking eyes. "Look me in the eye and tell me you didn't rape that girl."

He rolls his eyes, unable to keep the eye contact I demanded.

"Tell me you didn't slip something in her drink and brutalize her because she fucking rejected you."

He looks away. "She was a bitch, I didn't do shit she didn't want me to."

I laugh, the sound as feral as the look no doubt shining from my eyes. "I'm sure she wanted you to strangle her when she fought," I muse, the hysteria in my voice eerily calm, making him attempt to scurry backward. "And she definitely fucking wanted you to rip into her leg with your teeth when she screamed."

He shuffles away, working to stand but I push him back down.

"I could fucking kill you," I threaten. "Beat you until that fucked up brain in your head no longer functions. I could strangle you like you did her, but take it a step further and rid your body from the breath it doesn't deserve."

"What do you fucking care about some skank with a holier than thou attitude?"

"I love her."

His face twists in disbelief. "*What?*"

Standing, the sole of my shoe crushed against his crotch, I step harder, throwing more of my weight into it. He cries out in pain. "You *ever* touch another human being without their fucking permission, I'll fucking know about it," I threaten. "I will make it my life's work to destroy you. I won't rest until that's a reality. Am I understood?" I twist my foot into his junk, finding joy as he squeals in pain.

Stepping back, I glance around the now quiet bar, eyes watching on in a mixture of intrigue and concern.

"Ladies and gentlemen," I bellow, loud enough to be heard across the space. "This scumbag squirming on the ground is a rapist. He drugs women and brutalizes them. Don't be fooled by the pretty face, he's pure fucking poison on the inside."

Spitting in his face, I turn, walking from the bar without a backward glance to the man, who for most of my life I counted as a brother. I'm a coward, but not afraid to admit as I breach the exit, fresh air hitting my face, that I pray someone stronger than I am in that bar has questionable enough morals to put that motherfucker out of our misery.

Hand running down my face, I grimace. Looking to my knuckles, I stretch my fingers in and out, wincing. Blood seeps along my hand, pain throbbing in thick sturdy spurts. Shaking it out, all I can think is how I'd love to do it over and over again. Pound my fist into his face again and again until I'd shattered every bone.

How do you not see that? That your best friend is a monster. The worst kind.

"Fuck," I spit out.

My mind, like always, wanders to Zoe. I can't begin to contemplate what she's endured over the years. Since that single moment Miller placed his focus on her and decided her world should be decimated.

She sees a weakness in herself that saddens me. I wish she saw the fighter that I do, the one cutting through like shards of light through the cracked window of her soul. She's so beautiful; light and dark, whole and broken. Zoe Lincoln is a fucking warrior, and her heart sings to mine in a way I can't ignore.

Can I ask that of her? Ask her to move past this life *connection* we unfortunately share. Regardless of our innocence in this twisted fucking mess, is our relationship already doomed? How depressing to consider that we never actually stood a chance.

How fucked is that? As if love isn't hard enough. You find someone that chips away at this dominating muscle in your chest just for life to throw roadblocks at every opportunity. That's before this clusterfuck that is Zoe and me. How does love survive that? How does the most complicated of human emotion overcome *every*thing to prevail?

My greatest fear already is that she's surrendering to her fear. I know what she feels for me, even without her vocalizing it and I think it frightens her more than she'd care to admit. It throws doubt at her view of the world. The blacks and grays she's settled in are fading, giving way to the rainbow that is life and everything it has to offer. She just doesn't know how to swallow that reality. Not yet, anyway.

With everything she's overcome in her life, I think she's

afraid of loving someone the way she loves me. She desires it, she craves it, but even that scares her. I just have to hope against all hope that what they say is true. That love can conquer all.

TWENTY-THREE

Walking into Caffeine Coma, I freeze just inside the door. The background noise from outside fades as the door closes with a small soft thud behind me. The sound of my heart beat thick and heavy, echoing in my eardrums like the boom of thunder.

Bang. Bang. Bang.

He's standing, pushing to his feet immediately as I set foot through the door.

He doesn't approach. He's too considerate for that. He'll wait for me to go to him. And if I don't, I don't, and he'll accept that too.

Hands tucked into the pockets of his jeans, he radiates the uncertainty coursing through my veins. My feet take a step in his direction before I've reconciled it in my brain. Then another. And another. Until I'm close enough to smell him, to see the tired lines framing his eyes.

"Hi," he murmurs.

"Hi."

Pulling his hand from his pocket, he gestures to a seat. "Would you sit?"

Swallowing my hesitance, I nod, dropping into the nearest chair.

Confident that I'm as comfortable as I can be, he follows suit, sitting across from me. Elbows to knees, he leans in, eyes settling eagerly on my face.

"You doing okay?"

Am I okay?

Based on my tumultuous history with my emotions, most people would surmise I'm *not* okay. But surprisingly I'm not a puddle. I haven't reverted into myself and let this circumstance of my life beat me down, well not completely. I had my bad days, the days when I thought all was lost once again.

But in all honesty, I think I've come out stronger. Or maybe I was stronger before, so weathering this storm was easier than past experience.

Truth be told, I may be getting ahead of myself, it's only been a week since everything fell apart. Seven days since the greatest thing in my life was twisted and turned into something that should've sent me running.

Instead, I dusted myself off, with the help of Rae and Hannah, who turned up at my apartment about fifteen minutes after Tripp had left.

After unraveling and letting myself become lost in my head for days, I forced myself up. More than that, I moved past my need to hide. My need to cower into myself. Taylor Smith, the ghost, the shell of a woman I chose to be, disappeared. In her place, Zoe rose again. Something I never imagined happening.

Book club, Rake, I offered them my real name, told them I

wasn't ready to share my *why* and not one of them blinked an eyelid. In fact, they seem to have accepted me *more*. Likely they knew I was holding back, giving only the parts of me I felt comfortable sharing.

It took me some time to realize, but hiding, it only served to offer Miller more power. He can only continue to hurt me while I let him.

And I decide *against* that.

I'm done with that soul-sucking piece of shit taking my happiness with only his haunting memory.

Teeth pressed into my bottom lip, I nod, the gesture far from convincing. "Good days and bad. It was all a lot to swallow... I spiraled for a few days, lost in my head. But, I'm climbing out of the dark hole."

He picks at his fingernails, an out of character nuance. Tripp Tanner is self-assured, he's confident. Not here, not now. Sitting in front of me, shoulders hunched, he looks lost, uncertain. Rubbing at his nose, his fingers move to massage his eye sockets before dropping away again. "I can't change the past," he decrees, the defeat and regret in his voice as poignant as it is numb. "I can't even pretend that I can give you a life that will erase it."

I close my eyes against the sting of hope his words stir inside of me.

"I get it now." His head moves up and down. "Your want to change the past. To travel back in time and erase the moments that have caused you so much pain."

My jaw shakes with my restrained cries.

"I'd lay down my life to give you that, Zoe."

Dropping my face, I let the tears brimming in my eyes tip over, falling onto the knees of my jeans in thick drops. I watch the denim change color, the light wash blue darkening with the rain of my emotions.

"I'm sorry I spent the better part of my life friends with a monster, worse, that I didn't see it."

I shake my head, lifting it to look at him. His face looks like mine, a steady river of tears coursing along his cheeks.

"I'd kill him if I could." There's a venom in his tone that lets me believe his word. "I'd take *everything* from him, including his breath."

"Wouldn't change it," I scratch out, finally accepting that reality.

Taking his life wouldn't serve a purpose for me. It wouldn't bring me happiness or peace. He'd still be there, in my memories, where he'll remain always; dead or alive.

Head turning to the side, his palm massages his neck heavily.

"Your hand." The knuckles on his right hand are bruised, ripped open in parts, scabbed in others.

Dropping his hand from his neck, he looks at his hand, the thumb of his free hand brushing over the damage. "He deserved worse," he whispers.

A quiet calm passes between us.

My silence overflowing with gratitude but lined with a thick a layer of envy. What I'd give to cause that man pain. To connect my fist to his face so hard I saw blood.

Tripp's is different, maybe regret that he didn't push his pain further. Embarrassment that he let his anger get the better of him.

"Your dad," I cough out. "He was Miller's lawyer."

Not *quite* an accusation, but enough to let guilt cross his features.

"My dad is dead to me," he grits out. "Was the moment he chose to defend that asshole knowing what he did. I'm so sorry, Zoe, I—"

"Tripp," I cut him off. "You didn't do this. Any of it. You don't need to apologize for anything. What I said that day about you being a liar." I shake my head, disgusted in myself. "I was not in a good place. I meant none of it. I lied about my name, you lied by omission about why you chose to do what you do. Who would've ever known we would've crossed paths, let alone develop..." I exhale heavily, a humorless laugh communicating what I can't.

"I've lived a good life," he confesses randomly, a sadness coating his words. He feels guilty for that. Culpable that his life has gifted him more promise than mine. "I've never had an event, a person... upend my life so brutally that their actions have dictated every decision I've made going forward. I've never experienced something so traumatic that living seemed a chore." The color of his eyes has magnified in his distress, the glass of tears curtaining them, bringing out a blue like I've never seen before. "I've lived a *good* life," he repeats. "But through that, I've *never* felt happiness like I have when I'm with you."

My eyes shoot to him in shock, wide in surprise, making him smile. The gesture is still sad, not quite like the smiles I've seen from him before.

"It's true." He shrugs unapologetically. "I've seen the world. I was brought up in a happy home, even with separated parents. I was loved, I was cared for. I finished school to then graduate from the college of my choice. I've been in love. I've experienced some of the most amazing places in the world with some really fucking amazing people. None of it compares to my moments with you. I'd give it *all* up for sitting with you in this coffee shop talking about Harry Potter and fantasy baseball and the existence of magic."

He watches me for a beat, seeing my tears and smiling at the possibility of their meaning, of the emotion behind them.

"I'm not gonna pressure you to make a decision today. I'm not gonna ask you to forget about everything and choose me anyway. You've had enough decisions stripped from you without permission."

Massaging my hands, I duck my head, begging my eyes to refrain from spilling over once again.

"I am going to tell you this though..." He waits for me to lift my head, needing my full attention. "I love you, Zoe Lincoln," he declares softly, his tone anything but. "I love every facet of your warrior soul. Every reinforced wall of your heart."

Hand coming up to cover my face, I cry into my palm.

"From the very first moment my eyes saw you, I couldn't look away. You're beautiful and magnificent and everything magical in this world. You're no hex, dove... I've been enchanted from the very beginning."

I brush away my tears.

"I told you once that you were the loudest thing I've ever seen, even trying to hide... Whether you care to know it or not, you claimed every part of me from the start. I'm yours if you want that. *My heart*," he clarifies. "It's more than a little set on you. To love is to fear," he burrs. "We spoke about that, but I think I understand it better now. Because my greatest fear isn't about you breaking my heart, it's about trudging through this life with my love unrequited. The greatest tragedy. Knowing you'll love someone until the day you take your last breath while staring at the possibility of living that love alone."

I still haven't spoken. Too shocked by his declaration. Unsure on how to respond. In truth, uncertain on my feelings.

"I'd love to help you find the life you want to live, the life you deserve. Whether you feel it back or not, please know I'll love you the way you deserve. Always. Be it up close or far away."

Standing, he sighs. "Greatest decision I ever made was stepping into this coffee shop." He looks around, a genuine smile pulling at the corner of his lips. "Greatest moment of my life was being doused in cold coffee by the beautiful stranger with sad eyes."

Stepping closer, he pauses for a beat. "No one is strong all the time, dove. Anyone tells you different, they're lying. Weakness isn't a flaw, it doesn't take away from the strength in your person. Hardships are a fundamental part of life. Likely one of the *most important* essentials of life. Zoe, you, me, *every*one... none of us are born with an inherent force in their person. Strength is *learned*. Resilience... it's *learned*. *Your* power is honed, it's perfected *over time*. You only get there" — he moves closer again— "by *overcoming* adversity. How do you find it deep within your soul to persevere? You're pushed to the point where resilience is the *only* option. You *endure* or you surrender." He shrugs like it's the simplest of tasks. Decide whether you're going to give up or continue. "Every stumble you take is a building block to your strength. You fall. You get back up."

He listens to my silence.

"Like a diamond, none of us are unbreakable. Doesn't mean we're not strong. To get to our core, to the beautiful, shining being of who we are, we need to be cut and polished. The process can be violent, but the outcome is exquisite. Just like you."

He takes a step away, turning back to glance over his shoulder. "I hope it's okay if I text you. Like I said, I won't pressure you, but removing myself from your life completely isn't an option for me, not until you tell me it's a necessity."

I nod, agreeing without pause.

"Speak to you soon, dove."

I lift my hand to wave, afraid I'll beg him to stay if I speak. Afraid I'll plead for him to love me the way he just promised he could. But I can't do that, not yet, not until I'm confident I can look at him without seeing Miller sitting beside him, the unwanted invitee in our relationship. I owe him that much. I can't break his heart, I won't do it.

So I watch him leave the coffee shop, my heart screaming to follow him, my brain patting me on the back for thinking with a level head.

TWENTY-FOUR

Tripp: Book Club 12pm. Caffeine Coma. Order of the Phoenix. If you're around, I'll be there. Thinking of you, dove.

"How many book clubs does that mean you've missed?"

Dropping my phone onto the couch, I glance at Rae. "Including that message yesterday?"

She nods.

"Just two."

"Two more than it should've been," she murmurs, and I glower at her.

"Aren't friends supposed to be supportive?"

Rolling her eyes, she throws a pillow at my face. "They're also supposed to call you on your shit when you're being a wally."

My eyebrows pull together. "What's a wally?"

Again with the shrug. "An idiot." She sighs. "Babe, I love you, but you've been avoiding him and pining for him all at once. You're reading the books, *again,* in preparation. You get ready as though you're about to leave, then wallow on the couch when you chicken out."

I scowl at her for making embarrassment heat my neck.

"What's going on?'

"I was content in my life," I tell her. "I was comfortable as a ghost."

She's unconvinced, the singular raised brow communicating that well enough. "You weren't content or comfortable. You were hiding, existing for the sake of breathing. There's a *massive* difference."

"Don't be judgy all at once or anything."

Head lolled back on her neck, she groans. "I'm not judging you, Zoe. I would never fucking do that. Ever. But I'm telling you there's a difference in the life you were living and the life you actually want to live."

Hugging a pillow against my chest, I cower against the truth of her words.

"You can live your life by yourself, Zoe. You can float through your days content in being alone. But *friends,* your loved ones, they're the promise of that pot of gold at the end of the rainbow. Life is as unpredictable as a storm but in those bleak moments. In those days, weeks, months, maybe even years" —she shrugs— "the light at the end of it all, are your people. They're the fucking rainbow.

"And you're not gonna find a pot of gold and a dancing leprechaun at the end, you find us. Your tribe. The family you choose, because... those dark moments, those days when your certain nothing exists past the black and grays of the world, we're the ones holding you up, making sure you survive to fight another day. Life isn't worth it without someone to share it with, Zee. Fuck, you can cut Tripp out, you can push me and your other friends away, but what's the point. What's the fucking point when you can't sit in a coffee shop and talk about Harry Potter and magic and laugh about spilled coffee. What's the fucking point when you have no one to send you a stupid fucking meme that makes no sense, but you smile all the fucking same? What's the point if no one hugs you when you cry or cheers when you're winning?"

"You're my pot of gold?" I tease.

Another pillow hits me in the face. "Fuck yes I'm your pot of gold. So is Dex, just don't tell him I said that. So is Hannah, Quinn, even fucking Joanie," she balks. "And so is Tripp," she finishes softly. "In fact, I think he's the biggest pot you've got waiting there. Love is hard, Zoe. It's messy and painful, but it's also one of the greatest things we can experience. You can't compare it to *anything* else. You don't overcome what you have, to fall in love just to let it go."

"What if he breaks my heart?" I whisper.

"What if he loves you so hard you've never known happiness like it?"

She's right. I know that without having to think too hard about it. The biggest risk we can take in life is to *not* actually take one. To live in your safe zone, your comfort zone without dipping your toes into the unknown, without ever having taken a chance on yourself. How many people will tell you the greatest rewards are sewn from the biggest risks. And when you think about it, what risk is greater than betting on your heart?

My life has changed more exponentially in the last five years than anyone could have predicted. I've been torn down in one of the most traumatic of ways. I fought to survive, at times *barely* scraping through. I've been two people, two distinct personalities reflecting my before and after. I found the strength I thought was lost. I grew as a person; both as Zoe Lincoln and Taylor Smith.

Zoe Lincoln will never be the same person from five years ago. But can anyone really say they're the same person from five years ago? My before will never once again be my reality, but accepting that I no longer have to live in the suffocation of my *after* is a realization I never thought would be mine.

But I can.

I can pull the parts of Zoe that survived my trauma, I can take her, mold her with the strength in the Zoe of now and quite frankly, I like that version of me. I like her a lot. These past few months of my life have been some of my favorite. I've met some of the greatest people I know. I've developed friendships I'd long given up hope on finding. I fell in love.

Jesus. I, Zoe Lincoln, fell in love.

I smile without realizing it, my face warming at the *firsts* Tripp and I have experienced and how many more we have to go. That's not saying I'm not going to struggle at times, that I'm not going to endure through nightmares that will remain forever. Self-actualization is in reach and I'm more than a little dumbfounded.

Standing abruptly, Rae startles. "What are you doing?"

I look at her as though she should already know. "Finding my copy of 'The Half-Blood Prince' to make sure I'm caught up for next week."

Her face breaks open, her too full lips splitting into a wide smile.

"Or... you know the book back to front, you could just message him now..."

I look down at my outfit; my sweats, oversized hoodie, and Uggs. "Like... you *will* need to change first, let's at least give him the impression you're *kinda* not crazy."

Flipping her off, I move toward my bedroom. Changing my sweats for a pair of jeans and my Uggs for my black Converse, I keep my oversized hoodie.

Walking from my room, Rae hands me my book, turning on her toe in a pirouette to throw herself back on the couch.

Snagging my phone from beside her, I pull up Tripp's last text message.

Dove: Book club 12pm? Caffeine Coma. Half-Blood Prince. No stress if you haven't read it, it seems I've missed the last two catch ups. I'm thinking of you too.

Tripp: Dove. I've read every book in preparation for this very moment. I will see you there. I can't wait to see you.

"Well?" I look down at Rae, my TV remote in her hand, flicking through Netflix. "Hey, do you rate Noah Centineo? Lady parts are more my jam, but he tickles my fancy more than I feel comfortable."

Turning away from her, I glance at the TV. "He's a bit young," I reply. "But I definitely see the appeal."

"How old is he?" she challenges.

"Early twenties I think."

"No fucking way." She sits up, searching for her cell. "Fact-checking that. You look good." She pauses her search.

"Thanks. I'm gonna head off. Wish me luck."

She laughs. "Don't need it, Zee. You got love."

I scowl at her at the door, but she doesn't see.

"Twenty-fucking-two!" she exclaims.

I walk out the door, leaving her to her cradle-snatching dilemma.

He's not in Caffeine Coma as I walk through the door, but I refuse to let that alarm me. He said he'll be here, and I have to trust that.

"Swifty," Rake calls out, still preferring to use his chosen nickname and not my given name. I can't say I'm disappointed. I like it.

"Hey, Rake." I smile as I approach.

"How ya feelin'?" Leaning across the coffee-stained counter, he looks me over.

"Good."

"Does that smile you're wearing have anything to do with a certain lawyer that just stepped through the door?"

I spin on my heel fast, feeling Rake's chuckle against my back.

Tripp pauses at the door, eyes trained on our usual spot before scanning the space. His gaze falls on me a second later and his smile is instantaneous. The wide one, teeth on show, eyes dancing with the same happiness in his obscurely colored eyes.

We stand like that for a minute, separated by maybe five long strides. Last time I saw him, I felt the world stood between us. I could feel the weight of our misgivings pushing us farther apart.

But I felt raw, broken down by a power I'd let define me for years.

And he felt helpless, unsure how to navigate a situation so foreign to both of us a happy ending was nigh impossible. Confusion had settled between us so heavily, finding our way, *together*, would never have worked.

I had to find it in me to trust my heart, the way it had settled on Tripp Tanner even considering his connection to the single most harrowing moment of my life.

Tripp has had to come to terms with the fallout of his family, the people he knew and trusted, and the story he once placed his belief system in. He built his career, his passion on a fallacy. A large part of what he thought to be true in his world was the opposite.

Through it all, my feelings for Tripp didn't falter. Instead, they soared. I missed him in my life. He'd filled in the crevice in my heart only for it to feel twice as wide when I was left without him.

My heart, so used to feeling *nothing*, suddenly *ached.*

Lifting my hand on a gentle wave, he snaps from his daze, feet moving quickly toward me.

I wish he'd scoop me up in his arms, hold me tight and kiss me. Assure me that this life is ours. But I know that's not Tripp. As wild as his eyes are with love and lust right now, he refuses to be presumptuous. He declared his love for me, but I have yet to do the same.

Stopping directly in front of me, he exhales steadily. "Hi, dove."

I throw myself into his arms. It's the only thing that stops the tears threatening to spill from my overly watery eyes. Thick arms wrapped around me, he lifts me, turning us in a slow circle, face buried into my neck on a deep inhale.

"Fuck, I missed you."

Arms draped over his shoulders, I pull back slightly to bring his face into view. "I missed you so much."

"I'd really like to kiss you," he announces softly. "Can I do that?"

I answer with my lips, pressed heavily against his.

Hands tangling into my hair, Tripp deepens the kiss on a groan. His tongue strokes into my mouth, the desperate longing in my soul reciprocated through his touch.

I feel at peace in his arms, the feel of his heartbeat strong and steady against my own. The darkness I'd been hell-bent on residing in seeps away with every soft caress of his mouth, offering shards of color into my shaded world.

Pulling back, I smile up at him. "Can we talk?"

He grabs hold of my hand. "Yeah. Of course."

Settling at our usual table, Tripp chooses to sit beside me, not across from me and I'm thankful for the ability to keep his hand in mine.

"I still have a lot to work through in my life," I start. "I have days that are *so* good, I feel as though everything that kept me back is behind me. Those days I'm strong, I'm happy, I'm confident in who I am. But then I have days that are so black, I feel like there's no escape. Each one of those days feels worse than the last."

He listens quietly, his attention one hundred percent mine.

"After Miller," I pause. "After Miller attacked me, I was certain that love, friendships, and *happiness* were closed off to me."

His hand squeezes mine and I smile at him.

"I was wrong, Tripp. These last few months have offered me *so* much in the way of life. I felt unworthy of love and you showed me how wrong I was. I didn't think it was possible, but the hate and anger and fear inside of my heart is being replaced with love. I love you."

Pulling me onto his lap, he hugs me close. *"Dove."*

Hands cupped to his cheeks, I look into his eyes. Eyes that from the single moment they connected with mine I read their inherent kindness, the goodness within them.

"I used to tell myself that I must have screwed up pretty heavily in a previous life to have to go through what I did. But I know now that I'm wrong. Because whatever I've done to find a love like yours must have been pretty spectacular."

Leaning in, he kisses me gently. "Remember, dove. *Magic.*"

"You joke," I cry. "But it's true. What's in here" —I tap my heart— "for you, Jesus, Tripp it's not ordinary."

"Love *isn't* ordinary, Zoe. It's unconventional and remark-able and distinct to every individual person. The way you love me would be different from the way I love you. The only simi-larity for the two of us is that it's all-consuming. The rest is what makes it so perfect, how completely *dis*similar we love one another. Our strengths and weaknesses don't ruin us, they're what offers us perspective and protection; when I'm weak, you're strong, and when you're weak, *I'm* strong. We give and we take, and that's the extraordinary thing about love."

I stare at him, trying to determine if he's real.

"*Things* may take me time."

Placing a finger against my lips, he stops me. "We take it as slow as you need to go. My love for you has nothing to do with my need to fuck you, Zoe. I want to." He smiles, the gesture coy in the same way it's salacious. "But we don't need to rush it."

"What if I'm a dud?" I whisper, my cheeks shading with the mortification of the words that I just spoke.

Tripp's loud laugh tickles my lips, the color of my cheeks stretching all the way down my neck. "Baby." He leans forward, dropping his voice. "I've felt inside of you. I've seen you come. I've kissed you. Trust me when I tell you there is no fucking way that's a possibility."

Hand covering my face, I drop it against his shoulder. "There'll be days this will freak me out," I test, gesturing to our position.

"Then there will be days when we only hold hands."

"You're make-believe, I'm certain of it."

"Dove, I dreamed you up long before you did me. Waited my whole fucking life for you."

"Me too," I vow, sealing my words with a kiss against his smile.

TWENTY-FIVE

TRIPP

six months later

"The smell." She glances over her shoulder, chin rested on the fluffiness of her robe. "It's addictive."

Inhaling, she closes her eyes against the sun shining down on her face. I watch her unabashedly from my position on the bed; her bare feet on the balcony, face tipped toward the ocean. Bondi Beach screams with the incessant crash of waves, the sound of your favorite song on repeat.

I told her I'd take her to the beach, and she held me to it. Only demanding the best. I'd told her Australia, so that's exactly where we are. Where we've been for over a month now. And still, every morning, this is what she does.

"It's so free," she admires. "Chaotic, but free." Smiling, she wanders back into the room, eyes trailing over my naked torso.

Sex has been a journey. One we've enjoyed exploring slowly. It's actually been more enjoyable than I imagined, taking our time. I wasn't lying when I told her everything with her felt like a first. Zoe's put the affection and importance back into intimacy for me. I can't remember enjoying a woman's body more.

Her confidence is growing with every touch. She's coming into herself, finding her sexuality again and it's the sexiest thing I've ever seen. The tentative way in which she'll touch her own body, finding what sets her alight. The eager, albeit still hesitant, way she explores mine is like gasoline to my libido. It's better than I ever could've imagined.

Her nightmares are becoming less frequent. We can sleep in the same bed and more often than not she wakes peacefully, a smile on her beautiful lips.

Placing her coffee mug on the side table, she watches me, lust burning in my eyes.

"What are you thinking about?"

"You."

She grins, pleased with my response. Hand tugging at the tie of her robe, she loosens it, letting it fall open. It frames her body like a curtain, hanging loosely, the bright white a stark contrast to her sun-kissed skin. The tan lines of her swimwear are obvious; milky white against her now golden hue.

I knew Zoe Lincoln was exquisite but seeing her naked. *Fuck.* She's everything I'd dreamed of and more.

Narrow shoulders and a defined waist, her bones are delicate. She's small without being fragile. Not tall, but not definingly short either. Her boobs are like teardrops, dusty pink nipples, not unlike her lips, kissing outward. Her legs are long without being spindly, skin like fucking silk to the touch.

I could touch her all day, every day and be content in my way of life.

Dropping the material from her body, she climbs across

the bed, bottom lip caught between her teeth in coyness. She gets like this when she wants something specific but can't bring herself to ask. I imagine over time this side to her will fade as her confidence grows and I'd be lying if I said the thought didn't disappoint me. Her decorous nature makes my cock hard.

"What do you need, dove?" I burr, watching her swallow her lust down, savoring the taste.

"Kiss me," she says, her voice so soft I can barely hear her over the echo of the waves outside our window.

"Come here." I reach for her but she shakes her head.

"Not here." She touches her lips and my smile grows.

My cock, already rock fucking solid, pulses with her shy plea.

Standing, I trail my way around the bed, and she follows on her knees, moving toward me.

"Ass on the edge, baby."

Her breathing stutters, but she does as I ask, stretching her knees outward, opening herself up to me completely.

Dropping to my knees, I lick up her thigh. "Who's driving?" I kiss the soft skin of her inner thigh muscle, watching it quiver beneath my touch.

"Me," she shakes out.

Pussy glistening, I lick along it in one thick stroke, tasting her from the quaking pulse of her entrance to the very tip of her already swollen clit.

Head tipped back, she lets out a stuttered breath, hips bracketing upward, silently pleading for more.

She tastes sweet and salty, like the beach; untamed, a little chaotic but calming all at once.

Righting her neck, she watches me, eyelids hooded, green

eyes like wildfire. Tipping my tongue out, I glide it against her softly, a touch so gentle my breath on her skin is more punishing. A wicked sound of need and satisfaction breaks across the room and I move closer, my touch coming on heavier. Her eyes follow each and every flick of my tongue, teeth gnawing at her bottom lip, needy whimpers breaking from her lips, heightening my need for her.

Closing my lips over her clit, I suck.

She cries out.

She begs for more.

"Oh my God, stop," she whimpers, her plea a complete contradiction to the way her hips lift, grinding against my face, begging for more.

I can barely pull my tongue away, her taste addictive.

"Let me come with you inside." She pushes at my face and I growl out in protest.

She laughs, the sound more plea than humor. "*Tripp.*"

Standing, I lift her as I go, groaning as her legs wrap around my waist, the heat of her pressed against my stomach.

Eyes focused on my lips, wet from her arousal, she leans forward. "I'm gonna kiss you now."

"And I'm gonna kiss you back." I close the gap, sealing my lips over hers as I drop my ass down to the bed.

She breaks the kiss only to wrap her delicate hand around the thick line of my cock. Just the soft line of her hand feels like heaven, gliding along my skin in a caress that makes me throb.

Lining my thick head at her entrance, tongue caught between her teeth, she sinks down. Her tight heat pulsates against me, gripping me the entire way down. She lets me fill her completely, her clit pressed firmly against my pelvic bone.

Pausing, she adjusts to my welcomed intrusion, letting her body stretch to accommodate me.

"*So full,*" she revels, nipples hard, pussy clenching me in appreciation.

Leaning back on my elbows, I watch as she begins to move. The soft undulation in her hips grinding against me. Her hands glide up her stomach, grabbing hold of her tits to pinch her nipples on a broken moan.

I let her keep control, eyes tracking over her body as it moves on top of mine to bring us both pleasure.

Hands dropping to press against my chest, she pushes herself harder, hips gaining speed in a race to her climax. Jackhammering up, I grab hold of her ass with one hand, pulling her onto me tightly. Her movements stutter, breathing much the same.

Eyes opening, lids heavy, she looks down on my face, a soft smile twisting at the corner of her mouth. "Feels so good," she moans as I push upward, touching the inner most parts of her body.

Licking along her neck, I pause at the fluttering pulse point in her throat. It's strong, steady. I've learned over the months it changes when she's panicked. It quickens in a way that causes her to sweat, to shake. I can read her well enough, pulling back when I need to. Now isn't one of those times. Her pulse is thick, fast but not frightened. She's clammy, not perspiring with fear. Her body stutters with the feelings overwhelming it, but she's not shaking.

She begs me to go harder and I smile against her neck.

Legs wrapped around my waist, she tightens them further, wanting to bury closer. Connection, she fucking *lives* for it. Needing to be tied up in me, like I am her.

One hand braced into the mattress, I thrust upward, burying deeper with every movement.

"*Yes,*" she moans.

Pulling my face from her neck, I lean up to kiss her, claiming her mouth roughly. She kisses me back with just as much fervor, body quaking with the telltale signs of her orgasm.

"I love you," I confess against her lips.

It tips her over the edge, and she comes on a silent scream. Our kiss breaking, her neck tipping back, straining with the quiet sound.

Her pussy convulses around me. I growl, the need to come tightening at my balls. I flip her, needing more, dropping her back heavily against the mattress.

"Eyes on me, baby," I tell her, and she does as I say, her lust hazed focus on my face.

Hands to her hips, I tip them upward, thrusting into her body, riding out the tail end of her orgasm. I'll never quite get over this feeling. The way she grips me, molds to me. The sheer depth of what we share. It's more than sex, more than just a physical connection between two people. Our souls connect in a way that I've never felt in my life. It buries inside, the feeling like an elixir of hope and love and everything in between.

Her tits bounce in time with my thrusts, hands fisted in the comforter as I race toward my own release.

"Dove. Fuck. You feel so good."

"I love you," she breathes out, hips lifting in time to meet mine.

I come on a growl, hips fitting against hers as I spill inside of her.

Dropping to the bed beside her, I take her with me, her body resting atop of me. My breathing is heavy, like my heartbeat, physically moving her body in time with mine.

She mumbles something incoherent and I kiss her head.

"What's that?"

Lifting her head, she rests her chin on my chest. "I said, *that's* why you believe in magic."

I laugh, a rough chuckle bouncing from my throat. "Yeah, baby. If that ain't magic, I don't know what is."

"Mm," she agrees, leaning forward to brush her lips against mine. "I can't believe we have to go home in a few days."

"We could always stay?" I offer.

She laughs, rolling off me and moving toward the bathroom. "I couldn't. I love it here. But I'd miss Rae, Hannah and Dex too much. Plus, Rae's demanding my return, Potter plotting her death and all," she laughs and I smile at the sound.

A quietness hits her for a beat, not one of concern, more a contemplation. "I spent so long without people," she ponders, leaning against the doorframe. "The thought of leaving them is too much. Australia will always be here for us to visit." She smiles. "Friends and family are what are important."

Sitting, I grin, amazed at how far my girl has come over the past twelve months. When I met her, she was a shell, a beautifully, broken woman afraid of the joy life could offer her. She's overcome, she's fought, she's persevered. Zoe Lincoln turned the tables on her demons, the white flag of surrender no longer hers. No, that now belonged to the demons that haunted her for too long. Defeat was hers, as was her life, and she was intent on living it the best way she could.

EPILOGUE

Twelve months ago my world was bleak, shrouded in the black and grays of an unforgiving world. I felt older than my thirty-one years, and happiness was a memory I struggled to grasp hold of. My body felt like that of a stranger. My mind a prisoner to my own torment.

I won't ever forget that night, but it no longer infiltrates my every thought like a reoccurring nightmare. It may have taken me years, but I'm finally winning the strongest battle I've ever had to fight; to claim my mind back. Miller Jacobs no longer controls my life. His actions definitely affect the way I approach certain situations, but I've accepted that's life experience in general. It's not his power. It's not his influence. It's *my* experience, *my* decision in the way I go about *my* life.

I no longer *long* for greater justice for myself. I want it, but I don't *long* for it. I don't let myself *dwell* on it. I don't let myself think about Miller and where his life has taken him. I don't know if he wound up back in jail. I don't know whether he harmed anyone else. Hell, he could've been rehabilitated like our judicial system put their belief into. I will despise his existence for the rest of my days, but I aim to do so without craving further restitution. It only causes me more damage in the long run, something I vowed never to give him any more of.

I've found my place in the world. I was hiding behind a fake name, pretending I was coping. Zoe was always there though, parts of her slicing through the walls I'd had no choice but to trap her behind.

I have scars; both visible and not, but they're a part of who I am. I've learned that scars aren't ugly, they are not blemishes on your body or soul. They're fighting wounds. Trophies of what you've endured to get where you are, to become the person you were always destined to be.

Twelve months ago, had you have asked, I would've told you that my life had ended over four years prior. Now I'm living proof that to persevere is to win. I have friends that are so important to me, I'd count them as family. My work is flourishing. I have a man in my life who took the shattered pieces of my heart and painstakingly glued them back together. My heart is whole, it's beating in my chest, full of love and affection, overflowing with happiness.

I trekked over hell and torment to find the end of my rainbow. The pot of gold I found at the end made me richer than I imagined I could be. I didn't get there alone. I had a tribe of people at my back, pushing me forward, holding me up when I couldn't stand on my own. That only makes the victory all the more rewarding. Rae was right, sharing your life with people who cheer for you makes it all worthwhile.

ABOUT THE AUTHOR

A blonde. A brunette. A tea lover. A coffee addict. Two people. One pen name. Haley Jenner is made up of friends, H and J. They're pals, besties if you will, maybe even soulmates. Consider them the ultimate in split personality, exactly the same, but completely different.

They reside on the Gold Coast in Australia's sunshine state, Queensland. They lead ultra-busy lives as working mums, but wouldn't want it any other way.

Books are a large part of their lives. Always have been and they're firm believers that reading is an essential part of living. Escaping with a good story is one of their most favorite things, even to the detriment of sleep.

They love a good laugh, a strong, dominating alpha, but most importantly, know that friendships, the fierce ones, are the key to lifelong sanity and fulfillment.

facebook.com/authorhaleyjenner

twitter.com/authorHJ

bookbub.com/authors/haley-jenner

ALSO BY HALEY JENNER

Please visit your favorite eBook retailer to discover other books by
Haley Jenner:

The Leave of a Maple Series

Archer (#1)

Jake (#2)

Bennett (#3)

Maples, Strawberries and Fairy Tales (#3.5)

Luca (#4)

Toby (#4.5)

The Chaotic Rein Series

Tangled Love (#1)